MW01716350

SIMON PLASTER

SPOTS

A Tale of Star-Struck Misfame and Misfortune

Copyright 2017 by Simon Plaster

All rights reserved. Published by Mossik Press.

mossikpress@mail.com

Library of Congress Cataloguing-in-Publication Data

Plaster, Simon [9.12.2017]

Spots: A Tale of Star-Struck Misfame and Misfortune
by Simon Plaster

p. cm
ISBN 978-0-991-4480-9-8

1. Humor—Fiction.

2. Oklahoma, United States—Fiction.

3. Mystery—Fiction.

4. Commercials—Fiction.

I. Title10 9 8 7 6 5 4 3 2 1

Manufactured in the United States of America
First Edition

One of the things about the resilience of Okies when confronted with adversity is our ability to laugh at attitudes of others toward us while also poking fun at our foibles. Though SPOTS is set in a specific place at a specific time for literary purposes, none of what is herein dramatized actually happened and all the unfamous characters are entirely figments of the author's imagination. In other words, this book is pure-dee satirical fiction. On the other hand, if, say, executives of AT&T ever got a notion of making a hostile bid to take over the locally-owned Sonic drive-in restaurant technology for ordering food from parked cars, well, they'd better think again.

SP/ MP

SIMON PLASTER
SPOTS
A Tale of Star-Struck Misfame and Misf

spot: a television or internet commercial video message, fifteen to thirty to sixty seconds in duration, commonly presented as a dramatized skit.

SPOT #1

What Goes Around Comes Around

In the reception area of the OKC SCENE News Group office located on the near northside of Oklahoma City, Henrietta picked up one of several different-colored tabloid-size newspapers littered on a table next to where she sat, this one printed on grayish paper:

WEEKLY Stockyards City SCENE
Nightlife on the Wild Side of Town

BUMMER: BUTTS IN BARS BANNED
by
Sylvia Bird

Its front page and almost all of its inside content was identical to the other papers the News Group put out for OKC's multiple entertainment districts. Only a centerfold section called *WEEKLY Stockyards City VIBE* reported anything about nightlife in the stockyards area. With a sigh, Henrietta thumbed to there and commenced to read what she her own self had wrote:

GOODNIGHT, IRENE

As everyone in town is bound to know by now, last Friday night's KaraOkie Opry singing contest at Honky Tonk came a-cropper when the Texas-size beer joint burned down. Unfortunately, Honky Tonk owner and contest judge, V.D. "Moon" Mullins, did not survive the fire that got started when he his own self turned on the power to a big outside neon rainbow sign and caused an electrical shortage inside the joint. More fortunately, the power outage also resulted in failure of pumps to clear out a lake-size underground retention tank, so when the big dance floor collapsed hundreds of merrymakers who could not get out into fresh air were able to swim to safety by way of thousands of gallons of urine. Of particular human interest, a honky tonker by the name of Orville "Chad" Puckett did not know how to swim, but saved his own self by capsizing a boat occupied by his wife, Opal Puckett, who happened to be rowing across the underground reservoir with the karaoke machine operator, Wolfgang "Wolfie" Williams.

So in the words of an old honky tonk song...

The article was only the second, but likely the last one she would ever write about Oklahoma City nightlife, Henrietta reckoned. With Honky Tonk out of business and other Stockyards City saloons owned by Moon Mullins sure to shut down, she now felt anxious as a fryer chicken on Sunday morning of a farm family reunion. No doubt the OKC SCENE News Group boss man had called her in to tell her she was out of a job; and would have to give up her room at the Wobbly Boot Hotel provided by her employer due to his concern about her covering the rowdy stockyards part of town. Though she did not look forward to sleeping in her old yellow Checker of a car, even worse would be to go back to her little ol' hometown of Henryetta—that she was originally named for—with her tail between her legs.

Since high school, her dream had been to win one of those

Pulitzer Prizes for good journalism about something important, but after being in the big city for several months…"C'mon in, Henrietta," said the News Group boss man from the opened doorway of his office. "I've got an important assignment for you."

Important assignment?

The boss man set down at his desk and said it was an ill wind that didn't blow good in someone's direction. Years ago Hurricane Katrina forced the New Orleans professional basketball team to pull up stakes down there and temporarily camp in Oklahoma City; giving OKC the chance to prove it was a big league city that could and would support a team of its own, he explained. Now a whoop-ti-do to be put on by an Academy of Television Commercials Arts and Sciences had been forced to relocate from Las Vegas at the last minute due to a nearby Lake Meade drying up, even though **Budweiser** and **Coors** had got into a bidding war to fill the desert city's reservoir with beer in return for lake re-naming rights. "What goes around comes around," he said. "Years ago, Las Vegas tried to take our Cowboy Hall of Fame, and later stole the **National Finals Rodeo** from OKC.

"The so-called 'academy' hands out annual awards for the year's best achievements in TV commercials, and while watching television is not what I would call 'nightlife'…Well, the Mayor and other local powers-that-be are proud as Texans to be hosting the big show and are rolling out a bright red carpet for the event. Plus the **Sonic** drive-in restaurant chain has agreed to place a bunch of ads for their new Slurp 'n' Burp line of soft drinks. So I promised the Mayor I would assign all our reporters to the goings-on—from *Bricktown SCENE*, *Midtown SCENE*, etcetera—and publish for this weekend only a daily *OKC Tinseltown SCENE*.

"Mainstream media will probably fall for…" The boss looked at his computer monitor, clicked a keyboard button, and said:

"No recent up-dates, but *Hollywood Hourly*—a prominent show biz news site—reports, quote: 'Anonymous but credible death threats originating somewhere in the Pacific time zone have been directed at an un-named but important figure or figures if he, she or they dare to show up at awards festivities in Oklahoma City'.

"Stick to the awards and 'celebrity' personalities," he said, tossing in her direction a folder marked *PRESS KIT.* "Try to make OKC look semi-glamorous to our visitors, and vice versa. I promised you two weeks of employment anyway, including another four or five nights at that hotel. Next week, well, let's see how things go this weekend."

Phew! Henrietta was relieved of course that she would have a bed for at least a few more nights, but bridled at being told to stick to glamorizing TV celebrities and OKC. If she could figure out who sent those anonymous death threats, and who they were aimed at—what the heck—she reckoned that might be a good enough story to get her own self at least nominated for one of those Pulitzer Prizes.

SPOT #2

What's In <u>Your</u> Wallet?

De-boarding an **American** Airlines flight at Will Rogers Airport in Oklahoma City, Deano DeBoffo, famous Hollywood producer and director, immediately felt a bad vibe. He had been to the dirt-ball State of Oklahoma only once before, just weeks ago, to shoot a pilot episode for a potential reality TV show set in a small town, and that misguided venture had led to a run of bad luck. First, the pilot for *Beauty Parlor Gossip* lost out to another guy's *Barber Shop Talk* set in Ohio, in part because the *Gossip* idea had morphed into a documentary about three young local females who went missing, and from there into an exposé about women's underwear. Second, he had misjudged the talent of a local private detective named Maximo Morgan and cast the overweight doofus as star of a Hollywood gossip show called *The Fat Man*, which was an immediate flop. Third, he had crossed paths in the remote small town with an old chum, the famous investigative journalist, Shatner Lapp, and bought into Shat's idea of doing a sequel to the *Three Amigos* docudrama, to be titled *Return of El Guapo*, that went tits-up when Shat got put in the Nuevo Laredo jail for twenty-one years of unpaid child support. To top it all off, Mexican *federales* left his private jet in piccces, scattered across a tarmac, after tearing it apart in search of contraband women's lingerie.

So today he had been forced to travel to the Dust Bowl's capital city on a commercial flight, seated in the rear of the plane; and now wait in line for an ordinary cab to take him downtown on a make-or-break mission to salvage his career.

Three days ago, after watching TV into the wee hours, he had woke up in a sweat, with a boffo idea for an eight-part television docudrama. To make it happen, he needed to schmooze with the top dogs at Stanley & Stanford, and time was of the essence in his currently shallow financial straits. Bussing over to Las Vegas for a face-to-face was itself a pain in the ass, given that the all-powerful S&S agency was headquartered in Hollywood. But then, damnit, he discovered that the annual TV advertising awards wing-ding had relocated to—of all godforsaken places—Oklahoma City; and taken with it the multi-media conglomerate's big shots. These damned diversified agencies, Stanley & Stanford in particular, were harder to deal with than movie studios, but...Deano finally got into a cab and, as was his practice before making an important pitch, began to meditate: "Om...Om...Om..."

At the entrance to a ritzy Skirvin Hotel...uh oh, trouble already...a suited guy with a cord coming out of an ear held out a hand and asked for his credentials and security clearance. As he began to explain that he was a little under-staffed at the moment and had not got the memo..."Mr. DeVito!" said another guy. "Left home in a hurry? No problem. Happy to provide replacement papers for a famous celebrity such as yourself." Though ordinarily quick to correct the common error—like the equally well known actor, Danny DeVito, he too was short, bald and Italian—Deano let the case of mistaken identity slide. Fifteen minutes later, after getting a mug shot, "Welcome to OKC," the security guy said, handing him a bundle of papers, "which I am quite sure you will find just as 'sunny' as Philadelphia, if not more so."

Inside the eighth-floor Stanley & Stanford hospitality suite, he didn't even pause to nosh at an appetizing buffet, but made a beeline for…"Stan, my man, how they hangin'?" he said to Stanley. "Stan, my other man, how 'bout yours?" he said to Stanford. "What say we find a quiet place to chat. I've got a boffo project in the works that will knock your socks off."

In an adjacent room, seated across from the two agency bigwigs on one of two beds, he got straight to the point: "You fellas handle the **Capital One** account, right? Well, picture this: An eight-part television docudrama about the dangers faced by credit card holders on the mean streets of every big city in the world. Hmmm?"

"Could be interesting," said Stan Stanley, "but…"

"Lost and stolen cards are a big problem for **Capital One**," said Stan Stanford, "but…"

"It came to me in a nightmare: I'm walkin' through an urban maze and…Picture this: A big angry black dude mugs me. Next morning, I discover he's charged two-thousand bucks to my credit card for a zoot suit. Episode Two: I'm sittin' in a bar, mindin' my business and…Picture this: A good-looking hooker sidles up to me. Next morning, I find out she's put five-thousand smackers on my card for cheap jewelry. Episode Three: I'm…"

"The black dude is the hooker's pimp, right?" said Stanley, his agency's creative guy.

"Five thousand bucks for jewelry ain't cheap," his money-minded partner added. "Your card company is now out seven thousand dollars after only two episodes."

"What's your title, Deano?"

Deano paused for dramatic effect, stood up and said: "*What's In Your Wallet?*"

Stan and Stan looked at each other in stunned silence.

"Think of the advertising value to your client," Deano continued. "Hell, that movie—*You've Got Mail* —put **AOL** on the map. It still gets shown all the time on TV, almost twenty years later."

"You're suggesting a bold new primetime step in subliminal product placement."

"And sixteen hours of free network advertising airtime, just for starters."

"Hits the prime eighteen to forty-five age market..."

"...the way we hit on kids Saturday mornings with the **Mattel** *&* **Mars** *Chocolate Hour.*

"But no, Deano, our TVC star, Samuel L. Jackson is...Let's just say he's edgy and leave it at that."

"And expensive."

"Did you see Jackson go off on that TV entertainment reporter who made the mistake of complimenting him for a Super Bowl ad. He ranted and raved like a 'Black Lives Matter' maniac that the spot featured, not him, but another black guy. Implied, threateningly, that white people are racist because we think all black men look alike."

"Getting our female star, Jennifer Garner, to play a hooker would probably be an expensive proposition too."

"Television performance, especially in advertising, takes a lot more talent than movie acting, Deano."

"Even though most of the small-screen actors are cheaper."

"Hmmm," Stanley hmmmed, looking at Stanford. "If Deano could line up..."

"Hmmm," his agency partner hmmmed, with a thoughtful stare at his co-bigwig.

"We would get paid our usual fees for production and placement of spots."

"And get paid by both network and sponsor for the entertainment product."

"All I want is to get paid my usual fee for directing the series," said Deano, "plus a little something down the line in the way of residuals. They've renewed *Making a Murderer* for at least another season, and…Picture yourselves a year later, a couple of American Hebrews, walking down the Champs Elysees. A Hitler lookalike jumps out of the shadows with a bazooka on his shoulder and demands to know—in German-accented English—'Vat's in your vallet?"

"I like it. Gets your attention, but…"

"…needs an upbeat theme song."

"Okay, line up a cheap TVC star, but not one of ours," said one Stan. "Maybe that deep-voiced black **Allstate** Insurance guy who sounds like a troll talking from down in a well."

"Word on the street says that **Progressive** Insurance floozie is about to be out on the street," said the other Stan. "She would make a perfect hooker, and looks cheap."

When the two Stans stood up to shake hands, Deano—as short in physical stature as in cash—had to get way up on his toes to kiss each of them on an Adam's apple. He would have to stay in OKC for at least the day, maybe even get a room at the Y for the night, but hey: If he laid low, "Murphy"—the supposedly proverbial guy who made everything go wrong that could go wrong—wouldn't even know he was in Oklahoma for only the next twenty-four hours.

SPOT #3

Fritos for King-Size Dips

Henrietta parked at an unmetered curb right across from the entrance to a Skirvin Hotel, which was one of the benefits of driving an old yellow Checker cab of a car. In semi-awe, she looked up at the tall, old-fashioned brick building that—with three towers connected by two roundish ones—looked like a castle out of an old fairy tale book. Under an awning off to one side of the hotel entrance, folks were setting in a sidewalk cafe, eating muffins and drinking coffee. After passing through a carport and fancy big wood-paneled lobby that was at least two stories high, she her own self set down at a table in a large coffee shop and opened up the press kit the OKC SCENE boss man had gave her:

ACADEMY OF TELEVISION
COMMERCIAL ARTS & SCIENCES
2015-2016 SEASON
AWARDS

Welcome to the Academy Awards for the 2015-2016 Season:

In this, the 75th Anniversary Year of the first television commercial ("TVC"), the Academy is proud to present its annual awards ("Fritos") for excellence in the CREATIVE Arts and Sciences that are the sine qua non of commercial films commonly referred to as "Spots."*

Fritos are not to be confused with Clios, which are awards for ADVERTISING by various means, and recognize almost entirely only the business and technical aspects of making TVCs. Nor are Fritos* as limited as Emmys that salute only the whole TVC PRODUCT. Fritos* are more akin to Oscars, in particular the most prestigious Academy of Motion Picture Awards for the true TALENT—writing, directing, acting—without which television commercials, indeed television itself, would now be extinct.*

The background piece went on to tell that, at first, television commercials were just sales pitches made by people or illustrations, put on film and aired during breaks in entertainment programming. Nobody wanted to watch them, and nobody would have kept on watching them if ads—mainly in the form of song-and-dance routines, more recently in the form of humor—had not got to be entertaining their own selves. According to quotes of an expert named Jim Hall—who wrote a book titled *Mighty Minutes*—television did not become extinct because TVCs became a popular new "art form" that people wanted to see and hear. While back in the 1960s commercials took up nine minutes of each hour, nowadays it was twice that or more. Movies put on television were often edited down to make room. Super Bowl spots were said to be more popular than the football games their own selves.

Today the creative talent that goes into making spots far surpasses that which is displayed in most television programing per se—and that which is to be seen at movie theaters on the so-called "big screen"—bringing with it high-quality entertainment that is both free to the public and the engine of a mega-billion-dollar industry. Perhaps noted New York Magazine writer, Bernice Kanner, put it best when she wrote: "If Michael Angelo were alive today, he'd probably work on Madison Avenue." Recognition of TVC talent and performance is therefor both fitting and proper...

Henrietta skipped ahead to some photos of past Fritos Awards ceremonies. Twenty years ago a gal called Rosie the Waitress, the **Bounty** "Quicker Pick-Up Girl," won the Frito for Best Female Character. Back in 2006 **Capital One**'s Mr. No got the Best Male TVC Character award for his performance in *Close But No Cigar.* Last year the famous baldheaded **Farmers** Insurance Guy—dressed normally in a sport coat, tie and vest—was shown on a red carpet outside the Wonderland Hotel & Casino in Las Vegas, standing next to a formally dressed man who must have been a V.I.P. for...

At the sound of gals shrieking over by the coffee shop entrance, Henrietta looked up and saw...Land sakes alive. None other than Mr. Mayhem his own self—with a **Band-Aid** on his forehead and an arm in a sling—walked right in, set down right next to her, and...winked. It took minute or two for her to stifle an urge to ask the **Allstate** Insurance TVC star for an autograph, and get to asking interview questions.

"Oh this," he said, glancing at his injured arm. "I was texting and absentmindedly stepped in front of a school bus that sideswiped me before swerving into oncoming traffic. I sure hope those kids don't have cut-rate insurance that might not protect them from mayhem, like me."

And the **Band-Aid**?

"Ouch," he said, touching his forehead. "That's the unfortunate result of a recent, uh, personal encounter. Probably wouldn't be covered by my cut-rate policy even if I made the mistake of filing a claim. You yourself are not also married, I hope. And please, the name is James, James Mayhem."

After about another five minutes of mainly her own self not answering mainly personal questions put to her by Mr. James Mayhem, Henrietta said she had to go on up to the **Sonic** hospitality suite for a V.I.P. interview set up by her boss.

The **Sonic** chain of drive-in restaurants was a locally-based business, so from what the boss man had said, she reckoned its top executives along with OKC public officials would be pushing hard for maximum publicity about its famous TV spokespeople: The two guys who made up jokes on the spot, usually while setting in a car at one of the company's casual restaurants. That was how she found them in the hospitality suite: Setting side-by-side on a car seat, with the reddish-haired semi-funny one holding a hot dog and the other one a steering wheel.

She introduced her own self and explained that her name was now spelled with an i even though her original birth certificate had used a y to make it like her little ol' hometown, Henryetta, Oklahoma, that she was named for.

"We could use that," said the dark-haired one to the other. "My name's not Henry," his partner replied, "which is one of the reasons my mother never called me Hank."

"She never called you by any name, as I recall," said the wheel man. "Even your own mother always liked me better."

"My own mother, Wynona Sue, says you two remind her of the old-time Smothers brothers that she sometimes watches on the retro channel," said Henrietta. "One of them is normal and the other one…"

"Smothers brothers? You mean those two smart dudes who star for **AT&T** are copying our schtick?"

"No, the semi-funny Smothers brother is dumb. The other one just plays what you would call a straight man?"

"Our's is not an act; he really is dumb," said the dark-haired **Sonic** Guy, pointing a finger at his seat mate. "The humor is in the set-ups I feed him."

"Oh yeah?" said the dumbish-seeming one, getting up from the car seat in an obvious huff. "Just you wait and see who wins the Best Character Frito on Saturday night."

Left to her own self, Henrietta checked her press kit and saw that the "Frito" was a gold statue of a shucked ear of corn, and at the bottom of a page…

** Sponsored by Frito-Lay Inc. a subsidiary of PepsiCo.*

"Just exactly who are you and what are you up to?" said a voice from behind her. She turned around and recognized that it was the Mayor of Oklahoma City his own self, talking to her. "Thanks to you, our **Sonic** Guys are now furious at the **AT&T** Guys for stealing their act, and at each other for…You've got T. J. thinking he's dumb and Peter worried that he's not funny. Don't you realize these celebrities are creative artists, with fragile egos and short fuses? Or are you working for the opposition and intentionally trying to break up their act? I myself used to be an ad guy and well know how low some Mad Men will go to…"

Henrietta explained that she worked for the OKC SCENE News Group; had meant no harm; and further tried to defend her own self by telling the Mayor that from what she'd seen and heard it was powers-that-be pushing for one of the **Sonic** Guys to win a Frito that was more likely to ruffle feathers of the other one and get them to roostering back and forth.

"One Frito for <u>one</u> Best Character?!" his Honor said, looking like a little boy who'd been told by a big brother there was only one cookie left in the jar. "No, no, no, that can't happen," he then said, before wheeling around and charging in the direction of a man in a highly decorated billed cap and uniform, who must have have been the Chief of Police, Henrietta reckoned.

SPOT #4

Twinkie, Twinkie, Lesser Star

In her smallish room on the eleventh floor of a Skirvin Hotel in downtown Oklahoma City, Chloe "Clo" Courtney lounged on a barely queen size bed, munching a **Twinkie** and pretending to study a new TVC script titled *Blazing Chattels*. She was, as usual, in a snitty mood. For one thing, she had encountered her estranged twin sister, Florence, on the hotel elevator, which itself was bad enough. They had not spoken to one another in years and—with an armed security guard standing between them—rode upward in icy silence. To her horror, Flo also got off on the eleventh floor. To her severe chagrin, her la-di-da sister was escorted by the security guard to the end of a hallway, where she entered what was obviously a suite of rooms set up for schmoozing with important people. In other words—in addition to not being even nominated for a Frito—she, Chloe, had been subjected yet again to the humiliation of being the lesser TVC star.

Yes, it was possibly somewhat true that her own break had come, in small part, due to her physical resemblance to her already famous sibling, and even that little detail had cemented her second-class status in the eyes of TV spots fans and industry honchos. A *People Magazine* article, mainly about Flo, had compared them to two old-time movie stars—Olivia DeHavilland and Joan Fontaine—who once upon a time were also estranged sisters competing for the same slice of Hollywood fame and fortune. Fontaine, though a year or so younger and a later starter, won an Oscar; like Flo, younger by about five minutes, who had already won two Fritos. Yes, DeHavilland then screwed over her sister to get a supporting role in *Gone With the Wind* and later won a second Oscar for a starring performance in another well written movie, but she was young at that stage of her career.

Now in her forties, Chloe felt encircled by threats that her inept agent, Marty Lowry—now sitting at her feet, making a hash of painting her toenails—was not up to warding off. Yes, partly due to Marty's efforts, she herself had appeared in scores of TV spots, and was known far and wide as the "**Transgressive** Insurance Company Girl": Always dressed in white pants and apron as well as a blue headband, like Flo, the "**Progressive** Insurance Company Girl." But the scripts only required her to do such things as carry a firearm, literally shoot holes in stuffed burlap sacks identified by stenciling as other insurance companies' policies, and shout, "Bullshit! Bullshit! Bullshit!"

"Who writes this bullshit?" she asked Marty, throwing the latest piece of trash at her propped-up feet.

"I do," he replied, looking up from his assigned task. "It was, uh, part of the deal with **Transgressive**. I could write Shakespeare, but the client's targeted market is not exactly highbrow, and…Frankly, Chloe, you don't have quite the right, uh, voice for long speaking parts."

Voice? Who needed voice in television? She had the right facial expressions; "spoke" the right body language; and when caked with make-up, looked like...well, like Flo's twin sister. Acting in TVCs involved much, much more than mouthing the inane words penned by lesser talents.

"**Progressive** doesn't cover flatulent home owners who are also smokers," her hopeless agent unnecessarily noted, apparently in defense of his most recent script. "The risk of combustion is too risky. But **Transgressive**..."

Yes, yes, **Transgressive**—*The Goodhearted People for Hopeless Transgressors*—targeted homeowners and drivers unable to obtain coverage elsewhere: Prior convictions for arson did not disqualify anyone from buying **Transgressive** protection against losses caused by flame. Speeders, drinkers, weekend demolition derby enthusiasts and such were also warmly welcomed to join the **Transgressive** "family." One of the company's spots dramatized a bank robbery, police chase and apprehension of the driver of a getaway car, who was then cited for "loopholes" in his collision and liability coverage bought from another company. Policy premiums were pricy, and yes, **Transgresive**'s customers—and the bulk of her fans—though numerous, were distinctly lowbrow. Marty, a one-man band of sorts at the low-rent Mossik Agency, seemed unable to understand that what mattered in television commercial entertainment was not number of viewers *per se*, but placement of spots for a younger, more affluent market segment in time slots other than early Sunday mornings. In fact...

"Damnit, Marty, you never should have lined up that AARP Member Magazine interview. The writer described me as 'large' but not in context of stardom. My figure is still trim, damnit. It's the screens that have got large: Sixty inches or more, for crying out loud, and with horizontal high definition!"

"There's no such thing as bad publicity, Chloe," her so-called agent answered. "That's why we're here even though you were snubbed for a Frito nomination this year. A little sniping comes with the exposure. I'm sure you saw that Hollywood TV gossip show ambush of Flo, eating out of a supermarket cheese trough."

Yes, that was a good one, but...Through the years Chloe had enjoyed nothing more than seeing her high-and-mighty sister brought down a peg or two. Recently, however, she had begun to almost empathize with Flo's flailing attempts to fend off the forces obviously set on bringing her all the way down to earth with a cruel thud. Not long ago, big fat Flo was also caught on camera removing the battery from an adorable, ageless, look-alike "Flobot" brought in to take her place. Currently, an animated, talking cardboard box had begun to regularly appear in **Progressive** ads.

And it wasn't just Flo who was being pushed aside. The entire star system based on identifiable characters in integrated campaigns was under attack from all sides. Movie actors—some long dead, such as someone named Groucho Marx—were now appearing more often in TV spots, even as increasingly rampant product placements in movies were taking food from the mouths of TVC stars. Recently, the aging headliner of the World's Most Interesting Man campaign had been put out to pasture—which was no great loss—but now a boring younger so-called actor had been brought in to hawk Mexican beer to the so-called millennial market. And for crying out loud, the great William Shatner put **Priceline** on the map, but now **Travelocity** was winning market share on the cheap by using a garden gnome as its celebrity face! There but for the grace of God...

"There!" said Marty. "That ought to do for this evening's gala cocktail reception. Spots stars will all be in their regular costumes, so you will be wearing high-top sneakers, as usual."

Chloe ground her teeth. Desperate times required desperate measures, now, during the Frito Awards gathering of everyone who was anyone in TVC entertainment. Deep down in her hard, cold heart, she knew she needed to seize the moment: Either do whatever it took to relaunch her career in a new direction better suited for her currently under-utilized talents, or find a way to "remove Flo's battery," so to speak, then take her sister's place as the **Progressive** Insurance Girl! Stars were not subject to the same moral and ethical standards that applied to little people, which was the reason they were called stars.

SPOT #5

Heard It Through the Grape Fern

Henrietta spotted Ms. Peg Patterson, a local TV news reporter, standing over by a tall potted fern plant in the Skirvin Hotel lobby, talking to someone dressed in men's clothes and women's high-heeled shoes, with a brown paper sack over his or her head. No doubt he/she was an anonymous source such as Ms. Peg favored for the *On the Spot* reports she made on WOKC-TV. Henrietta her own self, along with an ex-boyfriend named Rodney, had briefly worked for the semi-youngish blonde gal—who some called Oklahoma City's toothier version of Katie Couric—but got fired for coming to the aid of an old woman Ms. Peg as much as accused of selling her missing foster daughters to an anonymous Iranian Pasha. That bit of "news you can use" was based on nothing but an anonymous neighbor claiming he had peeked through a knothole in a fence and seen someone, who might have been "Persian," call on the old foster ma.

Across the way, semi-hiding behind another potted fern plant, the Mayor, the Chief of Police and two other men—who looked almost like twins in their matching gray suits, white shirts, gray neckties and short haircuts—were in huddled conversation that she reckoned might be interesting. So she sidled on over and…

"…no doubt they're the dirty so-and-sos who sent those anonymous threats," the Mayor was saying. "In the **Sonic** hospitality suite, eating free hot dogs, they got into an argument with our **Sonic** Guy. I saw it with my own eyes and called in the Chief to…Tell them what you found out about those, those… those foreign bad actors, Chief."

The Chief took off his highly decorated billed cap and reported to the two other men that "the little dark-skinned bad actor" had admitted he was from a place called New Delhi, somewhere over in Iran, and that the other one had a blackish beard. "Both wear nerdy dark-rimmed glasses," he also noted. "So I called you boys from the F.B.I and Homeland Security to hurry on over here and export them back to where they came from before they have a chance to blow up the hotel ballroom and ruin the Fritos Awards wing-ding."

"You did the right thing, Chief," said one of the federal government men. "Highly sophisticated Homeland Security electronic sweeps during the past few years picked up security camera video of these two bad actors setting up a terrorist attack somewhere. One clip shows them fiddling with wires in an attic, until a female office worker spotted their ladder and interrupted their shenanigans. Another shows them up in the rafters of a big arena somewhere else, again fiddling with electronic gadgets and…This is Top Secret," he said in a lowered voice. "The bearded one, who goes by an American alias of 'Frank', made a trial run: Threw a bomb disguised as a basketball over his shoulder down into the arena. The little brown one, who goes by 'Charlie', looked down there, giggled, and called it 'a perfect strike'."

"And the F.B.I. has got 'em on film, getting pulled over by a state trooper one dark night, somewhere," said the other federal lawman. "The bearded one admitted they were setting up a national network of cells. The little Iranian one, who seems to think law enforcement personnel are stupid, giggled and actually bragged that their network was 'for taking down directions from the road, where you need them'."

"So we've had them under closely coordinated federal surveillance..."

"...hoping to catch them in the act of..."

"Catch them in the act?!" said the Mayor. "My God, don't you realize they are plotting to blow up the hotel ballroom when our **Sonic** Guy wins the Best Character Frito! "

Henrietta sneezed. All four of them turned their heads. When the Police Chief parted the stalks of the fern plant, they noticed her standing there with spiral notebook and pencil in hand.

"Don't you dare put these Top Secrets in a newspaper, you little snoop," said the Mayor.

"We'll have you in chains down at Gitmo before you can spell the word," said the Homeland Security man.

"Gimme that!" said the F.B.I man, reaching through the fern plant and snatching her notebook.

Henrietta had a notion they were humping the wrong leg. She her own self had seen video clips that were just like the ones the G-men had described, which were only TV spots for **AT&T**'s nationwide eye-phone system. What she wondered about was why the Mayor was so het up about the safety of only one **Sonic** "Guy" and not both of them.

SPOT #6

Uneasy Rider

With hard rock music blasting through hypersonic earbuds into her helmetless windblown head, Shirley Parker, astride a brand new gunmetal gray **Harley** *Freewheeler*, sped eastward on Interstate 40 at ninety-five miles an hour. A Saint Christopher medal dangled from a strip of bloody gauze tied around her neck. A speeding ticket—her third such citation since yesterday, when she left her cozy San Diego bungalow in a cloud of flying gravel—was clinched in her teeth. Her vanity tag, *RECKLESS*, along with a bumper sticker, *Stay Wild, Flower Child,* proclaimed the new attitude toward life that had come over her three months ago. Up to then—engaged for twenty years to a co-worker but unmarried at age forty-six and still a virgin—she had not thought of herself as an old maid, nor necessarily as a committed fiancee. To the contrary, as a prudent young woman, she had stored her eggs in an ice chest and set out to make a career for herself; never doubting that the right Mr. Right would come along and find her to be a desirable mate for the very reason of her professional standing. And sure enough, three months ago…

…She could tell right away/ that I was bad to the bone…

Contrary to later office gossip, she had not "stalked" Jimmy. Nor was she the person who assaulted him. He was already injured when she went into his hospital room for the entirely legitimate professional purpose of getting a well deserved WRECKLESS AGENT AWARD—not a single one of her car insurance customers had dared file a claim in 2015—that he would have presented to her at a banquet the night before had he not met with, well, with himself: Mayhem. Though his head was encased in plaster and his voice muffled, she had been able to hear him say that **Allstate** Insurance had long ago yanked his company medical coverage, and that his **Transgressive** Insurance Company policy for high-risk individuals had a million dollar deductible. The plaster cast extended to his torso and legs, but through eye holes, well, for Jimmy as much as for her it must have been love at first sight. His seductive unplastered hands were everywhere. But then…

I'm here to tell ya, honey/ I'm B-B-B-Bad/ Bad to the bone…

Her mother—in her youth a classic "One Date Girl" who didn't regularly eat **Kellogg's All-Bran** to guard against constipation—had strongly counseled against the torrid affair that followed her fated meeting with Jimmy, based only on her own unfortunate experience with an adventurous man. Forty-six and a half years ago, Shirley's father, a sailor named Leroy Parker, had boarded a ship in San Diego Harbor after promising to write daily and return to her expectant mother's arms when his duties on a distant shore were done. For thirty years afterward her mother had gone to the dock at sunset in desperate hope that his ship would come in. She'd received no word from him by mail, so feared the worst. "I know he's still over there on Coronado

Island," she still often said, "playing volleyball and cavorting on the beach with rich, blonde-haired debutantes." So naturally, "Don't make my mistake, Shirley," she had warned. "Do not pay that man's medical bills until he gets out of that plaster cast and into cement shoes chained to a post as your legal husband. And even then, to stop another woman from stealing your man be sure to use **Listerine** daily, and **Kellogg's All-Bran**. He is an incorrigible masher, just like Leroy Parker, with wandering hands and a wandering eye. He's a television commercial star, for heaven's sake. You can't believe a word he says."

B-B-B-B-Bad...

Her mother was wrong about Jimmy being "Mister Wrong," Shirley had believed. Her maternal worry about her daughter selling their **Allstate** agency and putting a second mortgage on the bungalow they shared was based on selfish concern for her own security. Probably Jimmy was still suffering from a concussion when doctors kicked him out of the hospital in the middle of the night two months ago. Probably he had wandered off in a daze, and possibly—God forbid—met with another mishap. What else could have explained why she had not heard from him, nor heard anything about him until last weekend?

Bad to the bone.

A *Hollywood Crier* column, *What's Hot & What Not*, was now seared into her bruised psyche: *Amid the many rumors of backstage backstabbing swirling in advance of this year's Fritos Awards there are whispers that* ***Allstate*** *Insurance will not bring back James Mayhem for another season if he again fails to win a Frito, as provided by his contract. His only chance would be to get a pathetic Lifetime Survivalship Award, for which the retired* ***LifeCall*** *Lady, Mrs. Fletcher, is favored. We caught up to the male falling star at Spago yesterday, skulking in shadows near the table of a certain well known* *married woman who was having lunch with her husband. Back on his feet, looking tanned, rested and ready, Mayhem publicly challenged the elderly Mrs. Fletcher to a physical showdown in advance of the awards presentation this coming weekend in Oklahoma City. Off the record, he said: "I'll come onto the old lady, lit up like a Christmas tree: Perfect shape, perfect hue, with a scent that will have her thinking she's making love to a lumberjack."*

Relieved but angry, Shirley had quit her starring role as Lady Macbeth in a little theatre production; officially dumped her fiance, Mike What's-His-Name; put a third mortgage on the bungalow; bought the hot **Harley** "trike" and hit the road. Now, with the Oklahoma City skyline in the near distance, she freewheeled her three-wheeled hog into a **Love's** pit stop to vent her bladder. Inside, however, even with her googles pushed back onto her newly bleached and spiked hair; her black leather vest covered with squashed bugs; her bare arm revealing her new tattoo—HOG WILD—she failed to turn a single head. A gaggle of gasser-uppers and quick-stop tinklers paid attention only to a TV screen mounted on a wall behind the check-out counter.

On the screen, "Peg Patterson, on the spot at Oklahoma City's downtown Skirvin Hotel," said a blonde woman, beaming at the camera with a blindingly bright, toothy smile. "Local police, F.B.I. and Homeland Security officials have refused to confirm or deny a hunch passed on by my confidential source that the target of anonymous death threats against an anonymous person attending this weekend's Academy of Television Commercials Arts and Sciences awards is likely either the well known TVC star, Mrs. Fletcher, formerly known as the **LifeCall** Lady who repeatedly fell and could never get up, or her Frito rival, Mr. Mayhem, famous for running into mishaps wherever he goes for **Allstate** Insurance. This is Peg Patterson, on the spot for WOKC-TV, with news you can use."

Damnit, Shirley didn't know whether to blame her clingy mother or her embittered ex-fiancé, Mike Somebody, for sharing her own "hunch" with the nosy TV news reporter.

SPOT #7

Where's <u>Not</u> the Beef?

Henrietta counted one, two, three...seven, eight, nine...thirteen, fourteen, fifteen...eighteen cloud-like chandeliers hanging over the fancy Fritos Awards cocktail reception in a Grand Ballroom of the Skirvin Hotel. But not everyone was dressed up, she was glad to see. Across the way, the familiar baldheaded star of **Farmers** Insurance Company commercials was outfitted almost like her—in jeans and sneakers, plus a regular old sport coat with leather patches on the elbows—looking ordinary as oatmeal. Standing next to him, Mr. Peanut...The chandeliers dimmed and the Mayor stepped into a bright spot of light up on a stage. "As his Honor of this big league city, it is my honor to officially say, 'Welcome' to our many visitors from out of town who have come here for this big league event," he hollered. "As one of our many Okie native sons who achieved fame and fortune elsewhere often said: 'We've never met a man we didn't like', to which I would now like to personally add: 'or woman I didn't love'."

Ha, ha, ha.

"Will Rogers may never have set foot in OKC, even though our big league airport is named in his honor, but his close friend, the famous aviator, Wiley Post, lived here and…" The Mayor looked down at an index card and said: "The only quote I have for him is: 'I cut the emergency switch just in time to keep Winnie Mae from making an exhibition of herself by standing on her nose'."

Ha, ha, ha.

"He was referring to the airplane he flew solo around the world, not to the one carrying Will Rogers that he crashed."

Ohhhhh.

"Yes, Will Rogers is long gone from us, but his spirit lives on right here in Oklahoma City. Let's all honor it by being good sports. While rooting for our favorites to win Fritos, let's remember: It matters not whether you win or lose, but how…"

Uh oh, the two **Sonic** Guys were up in the faces of the two semi nerdy-looking **AT&T** Guys, shouting at them. The Chief of Police his own self was trying to get between the two pairs of TVC stars, but now the **AT&T** fellas were taking off their eyeglasses and it looked like fist fighting was about to…Someone put a hand on her fanny, then another. Henrietta wheeled around and saw…"You're in my good hands, Miss Good-Looking," said Mr. James Mayhem, now sporting a fresh black eye, "with no **Allstate** agent around to protect you from mayhem, like me." She turned away, but he moved closer up behind her and stuck his head over her shoulder. "I'm your blind spot. My job is easy: I hide big things that go bump in the night. If you don't have a husband or boyfriend to protect you…"

She turned around again and told him to go bump a big thing against someone else, but…He moved up to her again and said: "I'm your hot water heater. If my pressure-relief valve gets stuck, you could be in danger of rocket-propelled wrecking balls from mayhem, like me."

That did it. Henrietta fetched a knee up against his "wrecking balls." Off he went like a rocket, holding his crotch with both of his good hands and howling like a wind storm. With pick-up lines such as he'd tried on her, it was a wonder James Mayhem—though semi-handsome—ever got through to a gal, but no wonder at all that he seemed to be so injury-prone.

Mingling in the crowd of cocktail drinkers with pad and pencil in hand, she caught a snippet of what sounded like an interesting conversation going on between two ordinary-looking senior-aged men—both gray-bearded—one with a name tag that said *World's Most Interesting Man/ 2008 Frito Award Winner* and the other with a tag pinned on his jacket identifying him as *J. Peterman/ Adventurous Advertiser & Aspiring TVC Character.*

"...carrying only my wallet made of chupacabra leather," the slightly older interesting man said. "Won it in an arm wrestling match with Fidel Castro."

"Fidel? Ha! I'm afraid that tale dates you, old man," said the aspiring character, "as did your mention of a commonplace wallet. For safe keeping of foreign currency as well as things such as, say, passports and little black books, I myself rely on a trusty, simple but eye-catching testicle sac snipped from between the sturdy legs of a Zimbabwean elephant in the Hwangean wild. XXX-large, shaved ever so slightly and stained for a more elegant look suitable for dressier occasions."

"Unlike ordinary people like you, I have no need for a passport," said the already famous TVC character. "Six countries recognize me as a national treasure. No matter where I go, it's the right side of the tracks."

"Ha! Nothing so uninteresting as that for me. One has not really experienced Marrakech, for instance, until he has probed deep into its wretchedly poor but quaintly unpretentious slums, where a man can be killed for slightly worn but handsome footwear such as…"

"My shoes get blisters, not my feet."

"…sandals, handmade and broken in by Tibetan monks. "

"My shirts don't wrinkle."

"How absolutely borrrring. I myself would rather be boiled in Papuan water buffalo lard than be seen in anything other than an artfully pre-wrinkled shirt, such as those made of handwoven human hair by the vestal virgins of the Lesser Antilles, singing delightfully erotic Calypso songs as they toil in the hot but refreshing Caribbean sun."

"My pillow is cool on both sides."

"Pillow! What a wuss. Give me a smooth rock from a Himalayan mountain stream, cover it with a Bedouin keffiyeh, and I'll sleep like a…"

"…discovered the Fountain of Youth, but I wasn't thirsty."

"You know, now that you mention it, I have often wondered at the stupidity of that endorsement of yours. Is the point of drinking ***Dos Equis*** to stay thirsty? Absolutely moronic."

Whether because of rivalries for Fritos or the reported anonymous threats—or both—tension seemed to be hovering over the ballroom like threatening weather. Over by his lonesome self, the **National** Car Rental Guy, who bragged on TV about how nice it was to be his own boss, was talking to his own self, looking as agitated as if he might be firing his own self. The new **Sprint** Guy was pacing back and forth with a phone to his ear, saying over and over "Can you hear me know?"—the **Verizon** tag line—like he was desperate to reach his ex-bosses at **Verizon** about something. Nearby, she overheard the sweet old **Frank's RedHot** sauce granny telling a red-faced **Chef Boyardee**—wearing a puffed up white hat and white apron—what she told everyone in TVCs, even the Queen of England: "I put that sh(bleep) on everything."

In search of something she might write up for an *OKC Tinseltown SCENE* that would make Oklahoma City look glamorous to TVC stars and vice versa, Henrietta moved on in the direction the smiling **Farmers** Insurance star and an old woman in a wheelchair—with a lumberjack's axe in her lap for some reason—who seemed to be starting up a friendly chat. When she got within earshot of them…

"Wipe that smirk off your face and the grime off those horn-rimmed spectacles of yours, you little smartass!" the old gal was saying in a semi-loud voice. "I am Mrs. Fletcher, not that new hussy who falls down for **Life Alert**. And you are a baldheaded, baldfaced liar. I fell down and cried out, 'I've fallen and can't get up!' for ten years, starring for **LifeCall**, but you insurance company bastards…"

"Oh, I know who you are, Mrs. Fletcher," the shortish **Farmers** Company star said, still smiling. "I came over to congratulate you for your well deserved Lifetime Survivalship Frito rumor. Regrettably, you didn't make it into our Hall of Claims due to the fact that, well, we know a thing or two because we've seen a thing or two—in your case more like two hundred—and after ten years of supposedly accidental falls…"

"Your so-called Hall of Claims sucks like **Electrolux**!"

Henrietta looked in another direction and…Land sakes alive. Standing against a wall was none other than the famous Hollywood producer and director, Mr. Deano DeBoffo, who had come through her little ol' hometown awhile back to make a reality show for TV. What in tarnation could have happened to make him his own self fall down to producing and directing thirty-second TVC spots 'stead of reality TV shows and docudramas?

SPOT #8

The Fault Is In Our Stars

Deano stood off to a side of the Frito cocktail reception, not entirely because he feared being spotted by his recent nemesis, "Murphy." Being surrounded by tall people made him claustrophobic, and he was on the lookout for the **Progressive** Insurance Company Girl, what's her-name. He needed to nail the big TVC star before bad luck had a chance to rear its ugly… Whale ho! On the same edge of the sea of people, thar she blew: Getting hit on by an old gent also dressed entirely in white. Two steps behind her, a shortish guy held a pair of what must have been her high-top tennis shoes. Obviously, he was her agent, just the guy Deano wanted to talk to. Cutting deals with ego-driven stars mano-a-mano was hard work, and demeaning. He sidled up next to the agent, discreetly pulled him aside, and introduced…

"Deano DeBoffo, what the hell are you doing here?" the agent said, before introducing himself as Marty Lowry, "a big fan."

"Got a major project in the works and a starring role for your lady-in-white," Deano explained. "Lookin' to cast her as my lady-in-red."

The agent swiveled his head toward his client, looked back and said: "Chloe? You're shitting me, right?"

"No need to play the coquette with me, Marty. We've both been around the block a few times. I'm here to make a deal for a streetwalker, namely your client."

"How real is your project?" the agent asked, still acting coy. "Clo's contract is coming up for renewal and...Now that I have your ear, Deano, I've got another client, not a performing artist, but a highly talented author of satirical novels. Now lives right here in Oklahoma City by happy coincidence. His 'tales' as he calls them read like scripts of integrated *Saturday Night Live* skits, all centered around a spunky small town chick. She's a newspaper reporter who tackles the absurdities of topical topics: Bigtime college football, presidential elections, climate change politics, inter-generational conflict, human mortality, etcetera. Great material for a 'boffo' TV sitcom or series."

"Sorry, Marty. Not interested in anything having to do with Oklahoma, a small town, or young female newspaper reporter. Take a tip from yours truly: For your own good, drop this so-called author like a bad habit, get out of Oklahoma as soon as possible, and concentrate on what's-her-name, Clo, right? Stanley & Stanford are backing me, Marty, my man, and I'm on a fast track. One way or another, by tomorrow—Saturday night at the latest—I'm gonna cast a leading lady and...You wouldn't happen to front for that black **Allstate** guy with the deep voice, would you?"

"No, Clo is my only performing artist. I mainly..."

"Too bad. We might have made a package deal. Soon as I get him and a female big fish on board—yours or someone else's—I'm heading back to Hollywood to line up a top notch screenwriter. Lights, camera, action by Christmas."

"Actually, Deano, my main talent happens to be screenwriting. Maybe we could, you know—as a certain other TVC star might put it—'bundle'. Know I mean?"

Deano felt comfortable with the guy, who was not much taller than him, and liked his hustle. Next he would be pitching his talents as stunt man and/or stage set designer, but…"What have you done that I could put my eyeballs on, Marty? This is a bigtime project we're talkin' about."

"I've got an almost completed script for a docudrama based on a bestselling novel—*The Platinum Loop*—and some other talents lined up to bring it to the screen. We've already shot a trailer and…"

"Okay, Marty, let's bundle," said Deano, extending his hand. "Deliver Clo and you get to write the script for my project—titled *What's In Your Wallet?'*—then we do *The Platinum Loop* together. Whatta ya say?"

"*What's Up With Your Wallet?* Great title, Deano. Comedy, right? Just my kind of thing."

Summoned by his client, the agent winked and…Oh no, at the sight of the little strawberry blonde newspaper reporter from that unlucky small Oklahoma town coming toward him, Deano fled into the assembly of mainly tall people.

"DeBoffo, my man," one of them said, "what the hell are you doing here: Auditioning for a 'short' part on the small screen? Ha, ha, ha."

Damnit. "Sammy, my man," he said to Samuel L. Jackson, the black **Capital One** actor he wanted no part of.

"You know Spike, right," Jackson said, referring to a midget-size black guy—also wearing big eyeglasses—who was with him.

Samuel L. Jackson and Spike Lee had edgy auras about them that made him feel uncomfortable, but…"Actually, I'm looking' to cast a black guy to star in a major project I've got going," Deano felt compelled to say. "Any of the bros lookin' for work?"

"Bros don't come cheap anymore, DeBoffo," said his man, Spike.

"What's in your wallet, Deano? I hear…"

Uh oh.

"…your credit ain't what it used to be."

"Mr. Deano," said a voice from behind him. "It's me, Henrietta, from that little ol' town where you…"

Never before so happy to be jumped from behind, he turned around and…"Henrietta, great to see you." After a moment's hesitation, he gave a big hug to the little strawberry blonde who had previously crossed his path like a black cat. "Let's find a quiet spot to chat," he said, nudging her back toward the edge of the crowd. "I wanna hear all about what's new with your mother, uh, Wynona Sue, right?"

Despite his determination to stay in a calm Om-Om-Omish frame of mind, Deano had a gut feeling that something was already going wrong.

SPOT #9

Stir the Plot and Hope It Thickens

Reckoning that a talk with Mr. Deano would be more like friendly chat than interviewing for the *OKC Tinseltown SCENE*, Henrietta put her spiral notebook into a back pocket of her jeans. "Wynona Sue is back to being semi-fine," she said in answer to him having asked about her mother, a hair cutter and styler at the Best Little Hair House back in her little ol' hometown, where the pilot for his reality TV show got shot. "She was disappointed, of course, that you didn't take her off to Hollywood, California in your jet airplane, but since you didn't go ahead and put *Beauty Parlor Gossip* on TV, I reckon things turned out for the best."

"Yeah, give Wynona Sue my regards," he said, edging away from her and looking over toward the semi-famous **Transgressive** Insurance gal, who was talking to Colonel Sanders. Henrietta her own self edged along with him. The famous docudrama producer/director had took a local Notary Public stamper and so-called private detective named Maximo

Morgan to Hollywood, and set him up as star of a celebrity gossip TV show called *The Fat Man*, but…

"I happened to cross paths with Mr. Maximo right here in OKC just last week," she reported, "and happened to be out there at Honky Tonk when he fell out of a chicken wire elevator just before the beer joint burned down."

"Why am I not surprised?" he said, looking at her, but continuing to edge away. "Nice to see you again, Henrietta, but…"

"So I reckon you're in town to kill two birds with one stone: See to it that 'The Fat Man' is alright and…What is it that brings you to this here TVC Academy get-together, Mr. Deano?" she asked, reaching for her notebook. "Have you took to making thirty-second docudramas?"

"No, no, I just dropped by to see a…a friend," he said, downright staring at the two black men he'd been talking to—one tall, the other short; both wearing big-rimmed eyeglasses—who their own selves were both glaring in the direction of Colonel Sanders and the semi-well known **Transgressive** gal known as Ms. Clo.

Henrietta got a notion that the famous Hollywood producer/director—and one or another of the black men too—might be sweet on Ms. Clo, and jealous about her flirting with Colonel Sanders. Hmmm. Could it be that the semi-elderly **KFC** TVC star was the "important figure" anonymously warned not to show up in OKC for the Fritos Awards?

Not that Mr. Deano would ever do such a thing, nor did she have any reason to think either of the African-American men would either. But love triangles could stir up heated emotions, Henrietta knew. Hopefully, Mr. Mayhem would not come a-courting the **Transgressive** gal who seemed to be at the center of manly attention. 'Course there were also other bad feelings in the air that might...Sure enough, when her lookalike sister and rival TVC star, Ms. Flo, walked by, Ms. Clo gave her twin a look that could have froze a side of beef.

Henrietta her own self had no sibling, but recalled reading about a reality TV series called *Evil Kin*. In one episode—titled *To Lose Is A Sin*—over-competitive family members were said to end up doing the unthinkable. In another one—titled *She Was A Good One*—two sisters grew up in a rivalry that was said to escalate out of control.

Hmmm.

SPOT #10

Great Balls of Fire! (Hiccup) It's Rhett!

As Chloe continued to sip a third Mint Julep, Colonel Sanders continued to look younger, and behave in a considerably more charming manner than he had during their one and only prior encounter. At last year's Fritos he had politely introduced himself, but only to then complain, absurdly, that her agent, Marty, had planted an *E News* story comparing her to the all-white, chicken-shaped hot air balloon featured in a **KFC** spot. An infringement on his brand, he'd had the nerve to claim. This year, however, well, the Colonel's repeated references to her looking "finger licking good" had almost made her blush through her heavy make-up. In a manner that was both bold—he was obviously wooing her—but courtly—taking his time to make the proposition, he now took her hand, discreetly licked her fingers, and asked if she had seen his performance in *Rub-A-Dub-Dub*, for which he'd got a Frito nomination.

"I wish it could have been you in the fifty-dollar family-size tub with me, Miss Clo," he blurted. "When I see you firing your pistol at those dirty burlap bags, I think of Scarlet O'Hara gunning down that damned Yankee who broke into her Tara plantation mansion to steal the family jewels."

Like every actress through the years, Chloe's dream had always been to play Scarlet in a reprise of *Gone With the Wind*: To wear a green velvet ball gown made of curtains. To dance away the night in a ballroom, surrounded by envious other southern belles. To be carried up a flight of stairs by a handsome rogue such as Rhett Butler. To be laid...She sighed. For a TVC star seen only in poorly scripted fifteen to thirty-second spots for a lowbrow insurance company, such an opportunity was likely to always be only a dream.

"Why don't we get our sponsors to join forces for an epic coordinated production," said the Colonel, still holding her still damp hand. "As America's most iconic people in white, we would be perfect in the roles of Scarlet and..."

"Her doting father, who..."

"...you could deliver your lines for **Transgressive** Insurance with a mouthful of **KFC** product, a bucket of finger lickin' wings on the kitchen table, next to a bottle of **Clorox** to pull off a TVC hat trick."

"And this time our side would win," said Chloe, almost swooning. "I couldn't bare to see Tara sacked again."

"Well, I dunno if we would want to go so far as to stir up..."

"Well, well, well, if it ain't TV's old finger lickin' cracker himself," said, of all people, the famous black **Capital One** star, Samuel L. Jackson. "Did you see me in that Final Four spot, telling my homeboys that chickens are no better than penguins when it comes to flying high, or for eating?"

"Still trying to cast a white trash woman to get into that hot tub with you?" said, of all people, the famous little movie director and also black **Capital One** star, Spike Lee.

"There could be a place for you in it too, Samuel," said the Colonel, "but only if you drop that surly attitude, and your asking price. For the record, Spike, I never officially offered a part in the **KFC** tub to Flo."

Flo? Chloe freed her hand from the Colonel's greasy grasp, slapped the dirty old **KFC** has-been's face, and turned to her agent.

"Marty! My slippers," she barked. "There will be no sloppy seconds tonight with this…carpetbagger."

"A wise decision, Chloe," Marty said, stooping to re-shoe her. On the way to his knees, "I have lined up a starring role for you in a docudrama series," he whispered. "A juicy one that's perfect for you."

Starring role in a docudrama? Before she could mentally process the startling new development, from behind her she felt…But no, after swiveling her head slightly, she sensed it was not Colonel Sanders, nor Samuel L. Jackson groping to find out "what she had in her wallet," so to speak. "I'm your blind spot," said her new admirer. "My job is easy: Hide big things that go bump in the night. That cut-rate **Transgressive** Insurance policy you have won't protect you from mayhem, like me."

She turned to a full frontal stance. "Why, I declare," she declared; "you, sir, are no gentleman." Her roguish rival, the swashbuckling star of **Allstate** Insurance TVCs—disheveled, black-eyed, fresh blood running from his nose, but still devilishly handsome—was now making a play for her. Again, Chloe almost swooned.

"And you, my dear, are no lady," he said. "We go together like a ham hock and sizzling fatback gravy, Clo. Let's, uh, 'bundle'."

"Marty! Make yourself scarce," she commanded.

As her agent inched away, Chloe scanned the room to see if James Mayhem and she were being watched. For a star of a competitive sponsor to turn his coat was dangerous business. Already there were rumors afoot that someone would get bumped off during this year's Fritos festivities, and in her mind there was little doubt who the victim would likely be: That Italian wiseguy—Marcarelli—who used to work for **Verizon**'s phone racket; making the rounds and asking, "Can you hear me now?" Trying to scare people into thinking they'd better pay-up to the big boss on the block who supposedly had all the connections. Now he was selling cheaper "protection" for the **Sprint** mob. Obviously **Verizon** had put out a contract on the double-crosser.

"Not here, not now," she hissed in answer to Rhett' s… uh, James Mayhem's behind-the-back but indiscreetly public proposition. "Come to room eleven-o-seven later, but make very sure no one's on your tail."

What a coup! With the **Allstate** box office heartthrob pre-packaged as her co-star, she could name her price, but not to the lowbrow **Transgressive** suits. After enlisting James and getting rid of Marty, she would no longer deign to appear in insurance company B-spots. With good material to work with…At the thought of reaching the stardom of, say, Jennifer Garner, in an epic advertising campaign such as **Capital One**'s classy *What's In Your Wallet?* Chloe again almost swooned.

SPOT #11

You've Gone a Long Way, Baby

After covering the big TVC Academy cocktail reception, Henrietta went down a grand staircase to the grand entrance of the Grand Ballroom that fronted onto Broadway Avenue; walked about a block up Broadway, and sat down at the counter inside a **Big Boy** diner. Though it was not all that late, a waiter named Charlie—according to what was sewed onto his apron—announced "Last call." At the end of the horseshoe bar, an overweight middle-aged man ordered a piece of pie and cup of coffee. A skinny teenaged fella across the horseshoe from him asked for a glass of milk. "And make it a double," he said. She her own self decided to have **Coca-Cola** on ice, then went to reconstructing notes she'd previously jotted in the spiral-bound book the F.B.I. man took from her. In her replacement notebook, she re-jotted:

*Hollywood Hourly, show biz news site…anonymous but credible death threats directed at un-named but important figure or figures who dare to show up at Frito awards festivities in OKC…heated TVC star rivalries going on…**Sonic** Guys fussing with **AT&T** Guys…and with each other about which one would win a Frito* *for Best Character...Mayor upset about only one such Frito to be handed out...*

Mr. Mayhem, and his hands, everywhere...hitting on women, some maybe married...arm in sling, bandaid on forehead...(and later, a fresh black eye)...

Mayor referred to only one ***Sonic*** *Guy in danger and needing F.B.I. and Homeland Security protection...???*

Since government suspicions about the **AT&T** Guys—based on video clips of likely just TVCs—were not worth re-mention, Henrietta went from jotting with a pencil to reviewing notes she'd wrote after getting a new spiral book at the hotel newsstand:

Sonic *Guys and* ***AT&T*** *Guys had to be separated...old men not so interesting but plenty quarrelsome...* ***National*** *Car Rental Guy having mental breakdown?...* ***Verizon*** *not picking up new* ***Sprint*** *Guy's calls?...* ***Chef Boyardee*** *upset with the elderly* ***Frank's RedHot*** *gal, (Ethel?)...old lady in wheelchair, Mrs. Fletcher,* ***LifeCall*** *star famous for saying, "I've fallen, and can't get up," mad at even mild-mannered* ***Farmers*** *Insurance star...called him a baldheaded liar...*

Mr. Deano jealous about Col. Sanders' attn. to Ms. Clo...also seemed anxious to get away from conversation w/ familiar looking tall black man and unfamiliar looking short black man...who later got in the face of Colonel Sanders...that then got slapped by Ms. Clo!... Mr. Deano less jealous?...Flo and Clo, tho said to be twin sisters (and looking the parts) didn't even howdy to each other.

Dang it, she had lots of leads for who might have made those anonymous threats, and who might be the targeted victim or victims, but nothing newsworthy to send in to the *OKC Tinseltown SCENE.*

"Wanna hear a joke?" the chubby man at one end of the diner counter asked. Henrietta looked up and saw he was talking to her. "Hot shot Mad Man back in the day: Thought he was always the smartest guy in the room. Decided to put together a TVC campaign for a product that didn't exist, yet. Did all the research. Designed a catchy logo and slick packaging. Got Bert Bachrach to compose a jingle; Sinatra to record it. Tried out the whole ball of wax on a dozen focus groups, who all raved about how good it was. So a pet foods company put out a line of dog food under the pre-packaged and pre-tested brand: **Nitro**. An astronaut launched the campaign from the moon. But **Nitro** was a flop. Wanna know why?"

"Why?"

"The dogs didn't like it."

"You call that a joke?" said the skinny teenager from his stool on the other side of the horseshoe counter. "Boom! Pet food company stockholders lost their life savings. Boom! All gone, and you can't take it back."

"Ruined my life too," said the older fella. "Women don't get jokes, in particular my mom, who signed up my two older brothers to be in a television commercial for a new breakfast cereal. The script called for my bros to turn up their noses at the product, but then try it and like it. They turned up their noses alright, but wouldn't try it because it was supposed to be 'good for them'. So one of 'em says…"

"No shit. Are you telling' me…?"

"Yeah, I'm Mikey, the three-year-old kid who got put up to trying the cereal by my brothers, and liked it. Ruined my life."

The now fiftyish Mikey went on to tell that his ad won a Clio back in 1974, and in 1999 was named by *TV Guide* as number ten on a list of best TVCs of all-time. Even as late as then, he said, a study showed that seventy percent of adults remembered "Mikey" from just a brief generic description of the breakfast cereal spot. But so what? He had been out of work for almost thirty years.

"Cry me a river," said the teenaged milk drinker, "and c'mon, Charlie, hit me again." He too had been a child star, he said. A whole year of his life had been recorded on thousands of yards of tape and later aired in dozens of TV commercials. His words, spoke from a playpen and translated into adult terminology became pop cultural catchphrases. His face was known all over the world. "Hell, I had my own changing table at Spago," he said, "but . . ." He took a big gulp from his re-filled glass. "Rumors that I was a milk-a-holic got spread around. Behind my back, the Madison Avenue suits started calling me an insufferable brat. So I'm sittin' at home one day, sweating out a Super Bowl bet, and…Mikey, they aired an out-take of me throwing a Category 5 tantrum about having to appear with a singing cat! The next thing I know, I hear myself say, 'I'm done. I'm out of here'. And that was it: Curtains for my career. **E-Trade** fired me and my agency, just like that."

"At least your agent took the fall with you," Mikey said. "Most of 'em turn their backs on a fallen star."

"**E-Trade** took the best year of my life, Mikey. And my agent didn't have to tell me I wasn't getting any younger. I told the suits I was sorry for being a brat, begged for a second chance…"

"You gotta be careful what you beg for in the TVC racket, my friend. I got a second chance with **Quaker Oats**—*Today's Mikey* was the title—doing the same **Life** cereal act as a college student, babysitting some brats who also didn't like the dog food. But I ate it. 'One taste, and you'll have a taste for **Life**' was the slogan. Now I can't get arrested in Hollywood or New York, and just look at me. You're still young, kid, but take some advice from someone who knows: Lay off the whole milk."

What a good "Where Are They Now" human interest story for an *OKC Tinseltown SCENE* article, Henrietta was thinking as she made notes, but…Land sakes alive. She looked up and saw that the heavyset, middle-aged Mikey had stood up and headed for the door, with a sign hanging on his chest: *WILL EAT ANYTHING FOR FOOD.*

She jotted: *Lots of old-time TVC stars seem to have showed up for the 75th Anniversary Frito Awards, some of them bitter about…*

"Have you heard about what Peg Patterson reported on the ten 'o clock news?" said the diner waiter, Charlie, as he picked up her glass and wiped the counter. "According to her highly confidential source, either that old lady who falls down all the time during television shows, or that **Allstate** fella who also seems to have a lot of accidents, is the likely target of death threats, and the F.B.I. doesn't deny it's true. I heard they are both up for the same Frito."

Hmmm? Though Henrietta hated to admit it, her ex-boss, Ms. Peg, may have got a good anonymous tip that would lead to a Pulitzer Prize-winning story. And, dang it, she her own self had run off James Mayhem when she had the **Allstate** Insurance TVC star right in her own good hands.

SPOT #12

Mother Wears Combat Boots

After cruising the streets of Oklahoma City all evening—plotting how to approach Jimmy—Shirley parked her **Harley** *Freewheeler* on a landscaped island in front of the Skirvin Hotel, where all the big TVC stars were said to be staying for the weekend. She looked up at the restored old-fashioned building. Yeah, Jimmy would be up there, probably just now hitting the sack, possibly not innocently alone. If she caught him by surprise…"Hey, you," said a dark-suited man at the door, "I.D. required to enter." She retrieved her wallet from a **Harley-Davidson** ditty bag and held up her driver's license. "I meant your Fritos credentials and password," he said, but…"Hmmm. San Diego, that's in the Pacific time zone," he then said, looking up from her California I.D. "Wait here. I'll be right back."

Damn! Realizing that anonymous threats against an important TVC figure or figures had set off a security red alert, Shirley ran to her *Freewheeler*, jumped onto the three-wheel hog and took off. Zigging north and zagging west out of downtown, into and through various suburban residential areas, she silently cursed herself for not foreseeing how tight security would be for the Fritos Awards. Now her identity and presence in Oklahoma City was known. What to do?

After traveling several miles from downtown, she wheeled into the parking garage of a Penn Square Mall, got hold of her cell phone and entered a number. *Buzz, buzz, buzz . . .*

"Click," she heard, followed by: "One, two…"

"Buckle your shoe," she replied.

"Three, four…"

"Open the door."

"It's Mother," the man on the phone said to someone who was with him. "She wants a meet."

"Open the door!" she repeated. "Immediately!"

Moments later, her contact answered, in code: "AC?QTBGLWMY."

Though not entirely satisfied she was not being followed, Shirley abandoned her trike, got on a bus and doubled back toward downtown. At a transit center stop, she waited until seconds before the bus doors would close, then abruptly exited the public transport. Walking eastward, she repeatedly looked left and right over her shoulders. A front desk clerk at the downtown branch of the local YMWLGBTQ?CA took her cash payment and—without asking for proof that she was in fact Jane Doe from Kansas City—handed her a key. She went to her second-floor room and immediately stripped down to her undies. Wrapped in a Y bathrobe, she then took fire stairs down to a spa. Inside a communal steam bath, she sat on a bench and commenced to casually whistle the tune of *M-O-T-H-E-R Spells Mother.*

Two middle-aged men, both also huddled in hooded bathrobes, hesitantly appeared out of the mist and sat down beside her. Their nervousness was more palpable than the steam, which was understandable under the circumstances. Publicly known as the two pathetically inept representatives of a fictitious insurance company—cast as straight men for the **Progressive** Insurance Company Girl, Flo—they were in fact hardboiled **Allstate** secret operatives, working under deep cover. Having served on the **Allstate** Agents top secret "Dirty Tricks Committee," Shirley was one of a select few who were privy to the company's back-channel codes.

"Are you crazy, Mother!" the hooded mole to her right hissed. "Clack and I are being watched night and day."

"Thanks to that fubar operation you put in play," said the other one from her left, "Click and I are living on borrowed time!"

They—code named "Click" and "Clack"—were referring to a failed "Operation Heist" ordered by **Allstate**'s real, never seen "Mother Hubbard," during which they were caught on security video in the act of trying to steal the top secret **Progressive** price gun. And what Clack said was true. Flo was onto them. They were living on time "loaned" for her wicked pleasure of watching them twist in the wind.

"We've heard—hell, everyone knows a hit has been ordered on some unknown someone, but we..."

"We never signed up for wet work, Mother."

"We want to be brought in from the cold, before..."

"That's why I called this meeting," Shirley lied. "Leave your Fritos credentials, your undercover kits, and keys to the getaway van at the front desk in an envelope marked for 'Jane Doe'; then make a run for it while you still can."

"You mean we're being put off the teat, just like that?"

"That's cold, Mother. The Company promised us starring roles in a new campaign if..."

"...and when James Mayhem gets, uh, terminated."

"I wouldn't talk that way about our star, if I were you, fellas. You might take a harder fall if, uh, something unfortunate happened to Jimmy."

"But Mayhem is the reason we're in danger. Your Madison Avenue ad spox stated publicly that Mayhem was 'gonna kick Flo's ass', damnit!"

"That's what put Flo on guard. That's the reason Operation Heist—and both of us—got blown."

"Something is bound to 'happen' to Mayhem. He takes too many chances."

"Wait a minute, Click. Don't you see? Mother has put Mayhem in the wind, and is setting us up to take the fall."

Shirley felt a sudden chill. **Allstate** had recently allied itself with **Esurance**, the very kind of cut-rate company Jimmy had warned of. Could it be that the real, notoriously conniving 'Mother' had also now decided Jimmy was unreliable, and "expendable"?

SPOT #13

The Guy Who Went Out Into the Cold

On her way back from the **Big Boy** diner to her parked Checker, Henrietta dropped into the Skirvin Hotel. Returning from a visit to the ladies room, she paused to look at some framed pictures and newspaper articles stuck on a corridor wall. All were about the history of the old hotel, and might contain some interesting background material for her reporting, she reckoned. One piece described the Skirvin, opened in 1911, as OKC's "Grande Dame" that through the years hosted—and served illegal whiskey to—Presidents of the United States and famous movie stars. Elvis Presley his own self also slept there. Another told how the old hotel went downhill in the 1980s, closed its doors in 1988, and went out of business for nineteen years. Mayors and other local leaders wouldn't give up on the city's grand dame, though, and ten years ago she was brought back to life looking just like she did in her prime, and even—some said—still haunted by a ghost.

Reckoning she had done all she could for one day and intending to go on back to her room at the Wobbly Boot Hotel out in Stockyards City, Henrietta headed for the front door. But a bright red grand baby piano had been rolled out of the hotel bar into the lobby and…*The minute you walked in the joint/ I could see you were a real big spender* a gal was singing to a bunch of gray-haired and baldheaded men circled around her. *So let me get right to the point/ You're in style when you're in*…**MURIEL**'S COMPANY! the men chimed in. *Hey, big spender, spend a little dime with me.*

HA, HA, HA…

"Hey, Anna, play 'Flick Your **Bic**'. You know…

Why just light up when you can flick your bic, the gal named Anna sang, as she played on the keyboard. *It's smooth and easy on the thumbs/ I'll flick your bic if you'll flick mine…*

HA, HA, HA…

About half the men were smoking cigarettes, which was an unusual sight to see, and all were drinking what looked like might be Martinis. *Kiss a little longer, stay close a little longer, hold tight a little longer….* **BIG RED** CHEWING GUM! they hollered. *I want my baby back baby back baby back*…**CHILI'S** RIBS!

HA, HA, HA…

They were carrying on about old TVC jingles, she realized, as one of them took to singing *I'm stuck on Brandy Ann 'cause Brandy Ann's stuck on me/ I'm stuck on Brandy Ann 'cause germs don't stick on me/ She holds tight no matter what, on fingers, toes and…. VD IS SAFE FOR EVERYBODY/ NOT JUST FOR THE FEW/ ANYONE CAN SHARE VD/ WITH SOMEONE NICE AS YOU!*

HA, HA, HA…

As the piano player started another tune, an old codger sang: *I wish I were an* ***Oscar Meyer*** *wiener/ That's what I truly wish to* *be/ 'Cause if I were an **Oscar Meyer** wiener...*ALL THE GIRLS WOULD BE IN LOVE WITH ME!

HA, HA, HA...

Five, five, five-dollar footlong, bellowed another as he spread his hands—glass in one and cigarette in the other—about two feet apart. *You can't go wrong with a five, five, five-dollar footlong...* CALL **ROTO-ROOTER**!

HA, HA, HA...

*My dog's bigger than your dog/ my dog's bigger than yours/ My dog's bigger 'cause...*WHERE'S THE BEEF?!

HA, HA, HA...

They their own selves were likely makers of advertising slogans and jingles from back in the day of the Mad Men TV show, on hand because of it being the seventy-fifth anniversary of TVCs, Henrietta reckoned, as she continued on her way. That they were jolly in the midst of all the friction going on between others attending the Fritos Awards events was a relief, in a way, but not newsworthy.

*I'm glad I'm not an **Oscar Meyer** weiner/ That's not what I'd want to be/ 'Cause if I was an Oscar Meyer weiner/ I would cease to be.* PLUNK YOUR MAGIC TWANGER, FROGGIE!

HA, Ha, ha...

Outside, Henrietta headed for her car, setting in a line of taxis right across from the hotel entrance. Another benefit of driving an old yellow Checker was that occasionally someone—currently a middle-aged man—would get into the back seat to be took somewhere. A woman about to get in behind him..."What on earth is he doing?" she said, looking upward. Henrietta turned around and—land sakes alive—saw that someone was creeping along a ledge on the...two, three, four, five, six, seven...eleventh floor of one of the three connected brick towers of the Skirvin

Hotel. A light came on in a window. Someone or something in the window moved… Oh no, the person on the ledge came tumbling down, down, down and…*RIP!*…tore right through a canvas awning before landing on a cafe table and plopping onto the sidewalk.

"Let's get out here, Maud," the man in the back seat of her Checker said to the woman, but…Though she could have used the fare, Henrietta reckoned she'd better stay put, to be of whatever use she could, and do some jotting in her spiral notebook.

FRIDAY

THE SHOW MUST GO ON

SPOT #14

A Morning-After Plan for Oops

Deano passed by yellow crime scene tape outside the Skirvin Hotel and burrowed through a crowd that had gathered in the hotel lobby for some reason. Inside an elevator and on the rise, he mentally took stock of his situation. Having bagged the cheap insurance company broad—Clo, Flo, Mo, whatever—his next priority was to nail the menacing **Allstate** black guy and get the hell out of "Dodge" with the critical starring roles for at least the first two episodes of *What's In Your Wallet?* casted. What's-Her-Name was too dorky to be a believable *femme fatale,* but in a low-cut red dress with a slit up the side, soft barroom lighting and fuzzy focus...The elevator doors opened onto the sixth floor, where a hallway sign with an arrow painted on it directed him to go right to see "The Good Hand People."

These insurance company types had no marketing pizzazz, he noted as he approached the **Allstate** Hospitality Suite's double-doors, decorated with funereal black crepe paper streamers. Inside, instead of scantily dressed babes offering glasses of champagne, he encountered a room full of stiffs, eating off a breakfast buffet, murmuring shop talk: "Too much risk"…"man-made disaster"…"predictable loss"…What a downer. But…

"How they hangin', my man," he said, extending a hand to the only big black guy he saw. "Deano DeBoffo, famous Hollywood producer and director, with glad tidings."

"Mine are hangin' a little low today," the guy said in a deep mournful voice that sounded like it came out of a lighthouse foghorn. Oh yeah, he made Samuel L. Jackson look and sound as unmenacing as Chris Rock. Perfect! In a whisper, Deano asked where and when he could meet with the guy's agent.

"What kind of heartless low-life are you, DeBoffo?" the black dude replied. "We lost a bro last night. This is a solemn wake in his memory."

Deano looked around, saw no coffin, but picked-up on the downbeat vibe. A room full of white bros and hos were in mourning, some with tears in their eyes, except for a bald guy wearing horn-rimmed specs, ratty sport coat and vest, up on his toes and in the face of a woman who was sobbing. "Save the crocodile tears, my Madison Avenue friend," he said. "We know a publicity stunt when we see one. This hotel has a policy with **Farmers**, and we have no intention of covering the cost of that awning your fall guy destroyed to make Flo look bad."

"That's my agent over there in the corner, schmoozing with The Man about a new leading character for **Allstate** TVCs, namely me," said the black guy, nodding toward a couple of jolly-seeming mourners. "I'll be starring as an uplifting superhero in a new campaign: 'Jim Dandy to the Rescue'. They've already come up with a classic rock jingle to set an upbeat tone. He sang: *Jim Dandy on a mountaintop/ thirty-thousand feet to drop/ He got a lady on a runaway horse/ Uh huh, that's right of course/ Go, Jim Dandy…*

Damn the luck! Deano felt like he'd got a kick to the crotch, followed by a tingle extending into his groin; the latter from a cell phone in his pants pocket, he then realized. The call was from Marty Lowry. "Deano, my man," said the agent/screen writer, "I guess you heard about Jimmy Mayhem's tumble last night. Well, heads up: That little strawberry blonde taggin' after you at the cocktail reception is sure to have overheard Mayhem proposition Chloe. And must have also heard Clo invite him up to her room."

So what?

Jim Dandy to the rescue…

"Don't you see," the agent said in a lowered voice. "'Someone' could be facing criminal charges, or at the least, 'bad' publicity."

Jim Dandy to the rescue…

"We need to put into play what you might call a 'morning after, oops' **Plan B**."

Deano again silently cursed the day that little strawberry blonde kitten first brushed his leg in that hick hometown of hers. With the deep-voiced **Allstate** guy not available…"Don't take this the wrong way, my bro," he said to the black actor, "but I don't see you as a 'White Knight' superhero. And it just so happens that I'm in the process of casting an African-American super villain in a docudrama about credit card theft that—what the hell—I might even dump the other major star I've got lined up to make you the superstar of…"

"You think I'm Samuel Jackson, don't you, DeBoffo. You say you're a Hollywood producer/ director, but you don't even know the difference between me and Samuel L. Jackson?"

"Well, Sammy…"

"Yeah, I get it. You're trying to steal 'Sammy' away from **Capital One**, to shoot a TVC 'docudrama' for, say, **Visa**, right? No way, DeBoffo. My people need a 'Black Knight' superhero, such as me: *Jim Dandy in a submarine…*

Damnit…

…got a message from a mermaid queen…

…he was screwed, and…

…she was hanging from a fishing line…

…time was of the essence.

…Jim Dandy didn't waste no time…

Deano headed for the elevator, cursing the bad luck that forced him to resort to some kind of morning-after **Plan B**.

Jim Dandy to the rescue/ Go, Jim Dandy!

SPOT #15

Go Out There And Break Another Leg

Henrietta followed temporary signs directing her to a Great Hall located between the Skirvin Hotel's Grand Ballroom and a Centennial Ballroom. A "Media Center" had been set up there due to arrival of a swarm of mostly national news people—drawn like flies to a feedlot—for a press conference. Dang it, she her own self had been right on top—or at the bottom—of a big story, but had missed the *OKC Tinseltown SCENE* deadline. Mr. Mayhem's fall off an eleventh-floor ledge was sensational international news and important locally. There was talk of canceling the Fritos Awards for fear that other TVC stars might be in danger. That would be bad for the glamor of OKC, and for her own self too, she reckoned, as bright lights for TV cameras came on and the Mayor stepped up to a podium.

"As his Honor of this big league city, I want to first offer my official condolences to the entire **Allstate** Insurance family," he said. "James Mayhem was a TVC character who acted not wisely but well, doing what he loved most: Drawing attention to himself by causing mayhem to others. Contrary to unfounded reports in some media quarters based in other spitefully overjoyed cities, all indications are that James simply stepped out last night—unfortunately onto an eleventh-floor ledge—for a stroll in our fine city's fresh wind. Possibly in a daze resulting from numerous prior unexplained slips-and-falls in other cities, he simply slipped-and-fell. That's all there is to it. OKC has filled a reservoir of blood, sweat and tears to prove beyond any doubt we are a big league city up to hosting the Fritos Awards. And by golly, as I am sure James himself would say about his downfall—no doubt after warning that anyone anywhere could be at risk from the likes of him—the show must go on!

"Our fine Chief of Police will provide details of this unfortunate incident uncovered by his personally thorough investigation," his Honor then announced, as the highly decorated Chief stepped up to the podium. "We have two eye witness to this unfortunate incident," he reported, "and both confirm what the Mayor just said. I cannot and will not divulge their identities, not because the investigation is ongoing—all the facts are settled—but because…" He looked over at the Mayor, who silently mouthed what looked like: "The show must go on," but…

"**Bullroar!**" someone shouted. A heavyset, middle-aged man pushed his way up to the front of the crowd. "**My client, the Transgressive Insurance Company, covers strolls on burning coals, swimming in polluted waters with piranhas, and about every other risky behavior you could think of**, he bellowed through a bullhorn, "**but not collateral damage to awnings caused by falls of rejected would be 'lovers'. Romantic courtship is way too risky—women say yes when they mean no, or vice versa—and our policy holder, James Mayhem, was notified of this loophole on numerous prior occasions.**"

Ohhhhhh the mob of news reporters moaned.

Another also overweight middled-aged man took the other one's place. "As local counsel for the **Progressive** Insurance Company," he hollered in a voice almost as loud as if it had come through a bullhorn, "I want all homeowners and car drivers to know that the recently lapsed James Mayhem was not a 'would be lover', but rather a known licensed-to-terminate agent in the service of the **Allstate** Insurance Company, whose mission—in their cold hearted Mad ad Woman's own words—was to 'kick the ass' of our TVC star, Ms. Flo. Any defensive action Ms. Flo may or may not have taken upon discovery of Mayhem at her hotel window was or would have been entirely justified."

Hurrah for Flo! Hurrah for Flo! Hurrah for Flo! a bunch of demonstrators chanted, as they marched into the Media Center, carrying printed signs saying *DEATH TO **ALLSTATE**!*

"Speaking as an **Allstate** agent," said a gal who had somehow got up to the podium microphone, "I demand that the **Progressive** Insurance Company be disarmed of its dangerous secret pricing weapon of mass seduction; and that the ho, Flo, be given a lethal injection for shooing James Mayhem off that ledge like a common pigeon!"

Boooooooo...

Land sakes alive. The two look-alike federal agents who had been tracking the **AT&T** Guys—both now wearing dark blind men's glasses—rushed up to the podium and pushed the gal off to the side. "The public is hereby warned that the F.B.I. and Department of Homeland Security have taken charge of the termination of James Mayhem by person or persons unknown," the F.B.I. man announced. "All others in attendance here are hereby ordered to remain calm and disperse immediately. I repeat, remain calm and..."

As one of the eye witnesses who saw Mr. Mayhem fall,

Henrietta was inclined to agree with the **Hotels.com** TVC star, Captain Obvious, who said on this morning's TV news that his fellow celebrity got out onto a hotel's eleventh-floor ledge for some unknown reason, fell off for some unknown reason, but clearly hit the ground due to gravity. That was all anybody knew, or would tell. The fact that she her own self might have seen a light go on and maybe a flicker of movement in a nearby window was not worth noting, according to the police detective she talked to last night and in her opinion too.

Unless and until something happened to another TVC star, dang it, Henrietta reckoned that her best chance of getting a piece put in other editions the *OKC Tinseltown SCENE* would be to stick to the subjects of celebrities and Frito Awards, like the boss man had told her to do.

SPOT #16

That's My Little Octopussy!

Chloe lay on her hotel room bed, exhausted after a tormented, sleepless night, but exhilarated by its outcome. For hours following the unfortunate incident involving that **Allstate** actor she hardly knew by name—innocent of any criminal wrong-doing but worried that justice might miscarry her off to prison—she had pressed her made-up face against the door of her room, looking through the peep hole in expectation of cops arriving to arrest her. At dawn, the sight of several suited men in the hallway had made her think her goose was cooked, but—lo and behold—they passed by in the direction of Flo's suite. Others followed throughout the morning and—praise the Lord—she realized they had come for her sister! How poetically just. She herself had escaped, at the very least, bad publicity that would have ruined her career, and would now be the obvious choice to take Flo's place as the **Progressive** Insurance Girl! After a few hours of beauty rest, her first priority would be to summon that little wimp, Marty Lowry, and...

Kock. Knock. Knock.

Chloe sprang from the bed. Through the peep hole, speak of the devil: There stood little Marty. She opened the door to let him in and…"Marty, you're fired," she said. "If you must have an explanation, the simple truth—be it the faintest of praise—is that I have outgrown you."

"Fired? But Clo…I've lined up a deal with a famous producer/director for you to play the starring role in a TV docudrama."

"Not interested," she said. "A posse of lawmen down the hall will have taken a rubber hose to Flo by now. When she's confessed and been dragged off to the pokey, I expect **Progressive** Insurance big shots will be knocking down my door before you can say 'Olivia DeHavilland'."

"Lawmen?!" said her ex-agent. "Are you crazy? Flo doesn't have to confess anything? The British and New York tabloids are going crazy with the story line of 'Pussy Galore turning on the **Allstate** agent, Mayhem; James Mayhem'. **Progressive** big shots—along with other bidders—are the 'posse', and Flo is now at the top of the TVC industry's Most Wanted Star list!"

Chloe collapsed onto the bed and put the back of a hand against her forehead. "But…but…but…that's not fair," she wailed. "I am the one who seduced the reckless **Allstate** agent. It was for me that he foolishly risked his life. I myself am the Pussy Galore who…who knocked him off."

"I know that," said Marty. "I overheard you put the make on Mayhem. And my man, Deano, happens to be on intimate terms with a newspaper reporter who was standing nearby. She's sure to have heard you make your play, so I've come up with a boffo **Plan B** to shift the 'bad' publicity from Flo to you."

Beginning to get the drift, Chloe rose from the bed. "And Colonel Sanders too," she said. "He was thereabouts, no doubt eyeing me like a plump…well, not plump, but more like a Spring chicken he wanted to get into a hot pot. With a little prompting of the Colonel…"

"That's my girl!"

"I will go down the hall and confess this very minute."

"No, no, no, don't do that, Chloe," her restored agent-in-good-standing advised. "There could be criminal charges, jail time and…all we want to do is spread hints to the media that you are a glamorous *femme fatale*."

"And let Flo go back to being big, fat boring Flo."

Knock. Knock. Knock.

"That'll be Deano," said Marty, rushing to the door. The even shorter little runt he had exchanged whispers with at last night's cocktail reception came in and said, "Sorry to be running late, Marty. Got stuck in a faulty elevator."

"Great news, Deano: Clo is all-in for for the docudrama role and **Plan B**."

"Whatever the plan is, I'm all-in too," said the Hollywood big shot, taking her hand in his. "In fact, now that I have personally met you, Ms. Clo, I can see you have the heft to carry…I mean I'm already thinking of featuring you—and no male co-star—in all eight segments of *What's In Your Wallet?*"

"What's In My Wallet? Starring only me? I like it."

"Picture this," the famous producer/ director said, as he rose up on his toes and put out both small hands to frame a camera shot. "You're sitting on a bar stool in a skimpy red dress, a classic *femme fatale*, looking good enough to literally die for. In the background, your theme song plays, or maybe you actually sing or lip-sync something along the lines of…*The minute you walked in the joint/ I could tell you were a real big spender/ Hey, big spender, what's in your wallet?*"

"Or even better, how about this?" Chloe said, holding up her hands to frame a close-up shot of her face: *Hey, big spender, is that my wallet in your pocket or are you just glad to see me?*"

"Well, like I say, we could lip-sync it, but you see, Clo, the point of the lyrics is…"

"You'll be world famous, not as Chloe Cocker, but as… as 'Octopussy'," Marty cried out, "the *femme fatale* who got Mayhem, James Mayhem, to fall for you, hard!"

Chloe again fell onto the bed, again put the back of a hand to her forehead, and literally swooned.

SPOT #17

I T'ought I Taw A Putty Tat

Henrietta consulted a TVC Academy hand-out to see what was scheduled for the morning. Down a narrow stairway to a basement—called the Skirvin Hotel's first floor, according to the press kit, because the man who put up the hotel didn't want it to be an "unlucky" thirteen-floor building—a sign on an easel said:

Academy of TVC Arts & Sciences
2016
Awards
UNDERCARD

Inside a smallish meeting room, only fifteen or twenty folding chairs were set up and only three of them were occupied: A middle-aged gal holding bouquet of yellow roses set on the front row, and two elderly gents set side by side about halfway back. Just as she her own self set down and took her spiral notebook out of a shirt pocket, a gray-haired man wearing a plastic green visor arrived, went to a podium, and opened a folder he'd carried in.

"Good morning one and all…four," he said. "The Board of Directors of the Academy has decided that it is fitting and proper that I—Managing Partner of the accounting firm of Dewey, Cheatham & Howe—act as both master of ceremonies and sole presenter for this undercard of the 2016 Fritos Awards." He paused, maybe for a welcoming clap that didn't happen. "On my way to the theatre tonight, I was stopped by a man on the street who said he'd not had a bite in days. So I…" He paused again, decided to turn a page in the folder laid out on the podium, and said: "For the TVC industry, 2016 has already been the best of times, and the worst of times.

"The good news is that the current presidential campaign of Donald **Trump** has demonstrated the potential and glorious future of the TVC art form. While it is true that all presidential campaigns are much like television commercials—comprised of personal puffery, unfulfillable promises, unsubstantiated slights of the competition—never before has a major campaign amounted to nothing <u>but</u> spots. And never before have TVCs been so successful, not only in marketing a product but—much more importantly—taking over airtime. The **Trump** campaign has virtually obliterated television news content, such as it was, and now represents the entire programing of one notable cable channel. Just imagine: Tonight millions of paying cable customers will sit at home, looking at an utterly still picture of Sean Hannity, listening to an unpaid commercial message delivered by phone!

"The other major networks routinely break-in on their regular so-called entertainment programing to pass along **Trump**'s 140-character tweets—essentially fifteen-second spots—or at least convey his bumper-sticker slogans by way of banners crawled across the bottom of the screen.

"Though the battle for airtime between so-called news, entertainment and sports content versus TVCs has raged for decades, no one could have predicted so sudden a breakthrough as has been brought about by the **Trump** campaign. A new era in which television content is comprised entirely of five to ten to fifteen-second TVC spots suited to the, heh, heh, 'spotty' attention spans of the prime Millennial Generation is closer at hand than we realized. Indeed, one can now foresee on the near horizon emergence of a new sub-*genre* of our industry's art form: TVCs advertising and promoting TVCs!"

After gulping down a glass of water..."Now for the bad news," the master of ceremonies continued. "As is the case in all revolutions, the **Trump** campaign has caused collateral damage. Specifically, I refer to the fact that **Trump** is not being required to pay for his spots. And given his usurpation of free airtime, TV ad buys by the Republican presidential campaign—that were expected to far exceed what was spent on TVCs in a futile attempt to elect Romney four years ago—are currently running at a rate of only twenty-five percent of what was expended in 2012.

"Which brings me to the bottom line," the senior accountant said, as he adjusted his green eyeshade. "In order to recoup in some small measure the revenue losses being suffered by our industry in this presidential election year, the Academy Board has requested, and both ABC and the FCC have agreed, that the actual Fritos Awards portion of Saturday night's primetime production will be limited to handing out only the few major Fritos of any public interest. The remaining three hours and forty-five minutes of booked airtime will be devoted to paid TVCs, which are, after all, what we are all about."

The emcee looked at his watch and—as Henrietta continued to furiously jot in her notebook—hurriedly went on to say that all minor Fritos for "animation, cinematography, costume design, editing, lighting, special effects, writing, etcetera, etcetera, etcetera" were thereby awarded by the Academy to the **Trump** campaign and would be shipped to New York C.O.D. "Oh yes, there's this too," he said, after thumbing through a few pages. "For the forty-seventh year in a row, the Frito for Best—which is to say, most maddening Jingle—is again awarded to *Nationwide Is On Your Side,* by Steve Karmen, 'King of the Jingle'."

Then off he went, followed by the middle-aged gal, still clutching the bouquet of roses, but now in tears. Out in the hallway, one of the two elderly gents who'd been at the awards ceremony ducked into a men's room but she intercepted the other one, to get his reaction to the TVC Undercard Awards. In answer to her asking, he identified hisself as a Robert Wrenn from Michigan, in town for tonight's Seventy-Fifth Anniversary TVC Hall of Fame induction, and to hang out with an old college chum named Simon Somebody. According to a printed card stuck on the chest of his jacket, he was a *1971 Frito Award Winner.*

"Won my Frito for an **Odor Eater** spot titled *Radical Chic,*" he said. "Absorbent shoe inserts became a hot item in upscale men's fashion after I got a prominent, and good-looking blonde Park Avenue socialite—wife of a famous white-shoe bandleader—to lick the feet of a well known member of the Black Panther Party at a gala charity ball. All TVCs directed at male consumers are basically about how to get the girl. You know: 'Shave with a **Schick** Quatro Titanium razor, head on over to the health club, and women will fall off the treadmills in a swoon'. But standards of good taste used to apply. Nowadays, for crying out loud, what creative talent does it take to make a spot showing a sexy woman, lying on a bed, cooing about a stash of **Cialis**?

"As for this year's Undercard Frito Awards, hell, back in the day, the term 'creative' meant artful composition of a substantive message," he said, "not inane twitter that's 'creative' only in the sense of being completely made up. Truth in Advertising rules were taken seriously back in the good old days, but now...Ah, Simon," he said, as his old college chum came out of the men's room. "Here's a guy who could have been an award-winning author of spots if he were not so inclined to get off message, and was not so longwinded."

The old chum was not willing to say what he his own self thought about the **Trump** presidential campaign winning all but one of the Undercard Fritos, but then added that Donald **Trump** reminded him of another cartoon character from the past known as "Tweety Bird." Though unable to make sense of that shortwinded comment, Henrietta reckoned she had enough news—along with a few quotes from Mr. Wrenn—to write up a piece that her boss might think was good enough journalism for at least a sidebar in tomorrow's edition of the *OKC Tinseltown SCENE*.

SPOT #18

It Takes Another Licking

At the sight of her swashbuckling would-be hero laid out on a sheet of cold stainless steel, all remaining vestiges of Shirley's anger instantly changed to feelings of remorse. The big lug looked just as he had at their first fateful meeting, except for absence of eye holes in the plaster that now encased his head, and extension of a cast to now also cover his arms and hands. No longer did she care about the Hollywood gossip column report of him dallying with another woman last week at Spago, then scheming to woo his Frito rival, that **LifeCall** vamp. And the current trashy tabloid speculation that he went out onto that hotel ledge to make whoopee with that overweight **Progressive** Insurance whore, while hurtful, was just that: Trashy speculation drummed up by those who wanted to sully her would-be hero's reputation. No, Jimmy was just Jimmy being Jimmy last night: No doubt desperately trying to live up to her image of him as a dashing TVC star, and deserving Frito winner.

If only he had explained his foolish insecurities to her, she would gladly have helped him remove that old whiner—the **LifeCall** bitch known as Mrs. Fltetcher—who stood, or rather sat in his way to winning the Lifetime Survivalship Award. Unless the Academy made a posthumous presentation at tonight's hall of fame banquet...Cruel reality struck Shirley's bereaved heart like a dagger. Without a Frito to his credit, there would be no re-runs of Jimmy's spots. Through the years to come, she and millions of others would see only that pathetic old woman—Mrs. Fletcher—pathetically begging for help after repeatedly falling down. James Mayhem would be as unseen and unremembered as her mother's girlhood idol, the movie actor, Gabby Hayes, who never won an Oscar.

She squeezed her almost-hero's encrusted hand. "Rest in peace, you big lug," she said aloud. "I've obtained Click's and Clack's undercover kits, the **Allstate** password for entry into that accursed hotel, and a nondescript **Chevy** van. Your snub shall not go unavenged."

Removing the bloodstained strip of gauze from around her neck, she felt a slight pang of guilt for having borrowed Jimmy's Saint Christopher medal on their first date, as he lay unconscious in the San Diego hospital. Leaning across his body to restore the religious talisman that would keep him safe in his afterlife adventures, she laid her head on his plastered chest and...Jesus, Mary and Joseph!

Shirley jerked upright.

Could it be?

But no, after falling eleven stories, not even the stout heart of Jimmy Mayhem could still...Almost certainly she had detected only the pulse of his trusty **Timex** wristwatch that through mishap after mishap had taken such a licking but kept on ticking.

On the other hand, one should not too rashly leap to conclusions in situations such as this.

After taking a nail file from her *Harley Hog* handbag, Shirley began to chip, chip, chip at the hardened shroud. Chip, chip, chip, chip, chip, chip, chip...

Finally, she broke through a soft spot covering the big lug's lower torso. Praying that she would feel a real pulse, she plunged a hand through the opening and...Jesus, Mary and Joseph!

She had heard that hair and nails continued to grow in the afterlife, but never...Jimmy's driver's license had been revoked, and along with it, thankfully, so had any rash donation of body parts that might have resulted in a fatal post-mishap mishap.

To assure her would-be hero's full recovery, Shirley immediately began rigorous vital organ resuscitation.

SPOT #19

Mumday, Mumday/Can't Trust That Day

Back in the Skirvin Hotel lobby, Henrietta noticed that her mother, Wynona Sue, had called her eye-phone: "Henrietta, I am your M-O-T-H-E-R, in case you've forgot," her message said. "Why didn't you tell me those Fritos were being handed out in Oklahoma City? You know how much William Shatner has always meant to me. Call back ASAP!" Dang it, Mr. Shatner was scheduled to be the presenter of a Lifetime Survivalship Frito tonight at a gala TVC Hall of Fame induction banquet, and her mother—a big fan of the "sexy" **Priceline** star—would no doubt be wanting to make the ninety-minute drive from her little ol' hometown to attend.

Henrietta was only semi-sorry to have to call back and tell Wynona Sue that due to anonymous threats against possibly multiple TVC figures, security in and around the Skirvin Hotel was tight as a wet boot and bound to get tighter after what happened to Mr. Mayhem.

"Well, I should think so," her mother replied. "That pointy-eared Doctor Spock has been trying to get rid of Bill for years."

Mr. Nimoy, who played plain ol' "Spock" in the *Star Trek* movies and had appeared in some **Priceline** TVCs with the ex-"Captain Kirk," died more than a year ago, Henrietta pointed out, but...

"That 'name your price' hussy, 'Naomi Price', is still on the prowl," said her mother. "She's a kung-food expert, Henrietta. Tonight could well be the last chance I will ever have to see Bill briefly in living flesh."

She tried to explain to her mother that no one who didn't have credentials and know a password would be able to get past security guards and into the formal ceremony, but…

"Henrietta, you know very well everyone says we look like twin sisters when I fix my hair like yours," Wynona Sue replied, semi-accurately. "I've brought along my Cinderella wedding dress that the online **Disney** store won't take back."

<u>Brought</u> along a dress? Oh no.

"I'm outside the hotel where Bill will be doing his thing, but they won't let me in unless I have false papers proving I am you, a newspaper reporter."

Outside the hotel? Dang!

"What about Professor Lehough?" Henrietta asked, referring to her mother's still newish third husband. "There's no way he could be made up to look…"

"I told him me and you were going to an opera show. He doesn't know about Bill, and what happens in OKC stays in OKC."

With a bad feeling that Wynona Sue, as was her habit, would likely cause an embarrassment if she got into the Hall of Fame induction banquet, Henrietta fibbed that she was in the middle of an important interview at the moment and would have to call back, but…

"Psst! Would you mind stepping outside?" someone behind her semi-whispered. She turned around and…"Henrietta, right? I need to talk to you about an important confidential matter," said Mr. Deano.

Uh oh. Contrary to what she had told the famous Hollywood producer/ director last night at the cocktail reception, Wynona Sue was not getting along "just fine," as far as regard for him was concerned. Since being the semi-moderator of his pilot for a reality TV show but not getting took to Hollywood, California on his private jet airplane, her mother had made a practice of still calling about every other day to rant about "that double-crossing little runt." But seeing as how he had on his mind an important confidential matter that might be newsworthy…

Outside under the hotel carport—with Wynona Sue nowhere in sight, thankfully—Mr. Deano seemed anxious as a broody hen. "Henrietta," he said, "I'm trying to hatch a boffo project—an eight-part TV docudrama starring Clo, the **Transgressive** Insurance Company broad—so I am begging you not to put anything in a newspaper about, you know, what you overheard Clo say last night to that guy, Mayhem. Mum's the word, okay?"

Since she didn't rightly recall overhearing anything said by Ms. Clo to Mr. Mayhem—but reckoned it was likely something along the lines of "keep your good hands off the goods"—Henrietta agreed not to write about it.

"'Cause, you know, Clo inviting Mayhem to come up to her eleventh-floor room—number eleven-o-seven, to be exact—might make it look like she had something to do with him getting pushed off that ledge," the famous Hollywood producer/director said.

Hmmm. An invitation from Ms. Clo might explain why

James Mayhem went up to the eleventh floor alright, but since she her own self had seen that he was not "pushed" off the ledge, she told Mr. Deano not to worry about her telling any sensational gossip about his docudrama star.

He seemed unhappy; then more so when Wynona Sue, wearing a big hat, came up beside them, took off her dark glasses and gave him the stink eye.

SPOT #20

Br'er Rabbit Uses His Head 'Stead of His Foots

At the sight of that small town hairdresser, Wynona Sue, standing beside him, Deano's better judgement told him to abort Marty Lowry's cockamamie **Plan B** and hotfoot back inside the hotel. On the other hand, he recalled a kindly uncle often saying: "You can't run away from trouble; there's no place that far." Most of his past successes had resulted from exercise of bad judgement, he also recalled. And as the middle-aged wannabe star went on to tear him a new one, he had to admit she was right: He should have followed the original *Beauty Parlor Gossip* reality show script that semi-featured her. He would have been better off all around to have taken her to Hollywood on his jet instead of the fat man, Maximo Morgan. And anyway, to seal the deal with the TVC star handpicked by Stanley & Stanford, he needed the mother to help him get her daughter to feed Clo's hunger for notoriety that Marty Lowry had whetted.

"I might have a spot in a docudrama for a fiery *femme fatale* like you, Wynona Sue," he said, as he steered her and her look-alike daughter—both strawberry blondes—over to where workmen were installing a new awning. "The agency big shots are set on starring Clo, but bad publicity..."

"Clo? You mean that overweight insurance company floozie that it would take two dogs to bark at?" said the admittedly petite hairdresser. "There's not a screen at the TV store with a big enough loop to rope her."

Deano looked upward and said, "Yep, that would be Clo's room, number eleven-o-seven, directly in the line of flight of Mayhem's fall." Then he looked downward, stooped and... "Hello, what's this?"

"It's a scrap of pink lace. I my own self have a French baby-doll outfit of the same material, but in red."

"Oh m'gosh," he said, holding out to the daughter evidence her own mother had identified. "This matches the negligee Clo had on this morning in her room—number eleven-o-seven—when I went to comfort her. Mayhem must have grabbed it when she... Please, Henrietta, don't make a big important story out of this... this coincidence."

"Henrietta has to write a big important story if she's ever going to win one of those Wurlitzer Prizes," said the mother. "Her potential is my passion."

"And there's a legend about this old hotel being haunted by the ghost of a woman named Effie, who jumped—or was pushed—to her death, right about here, where Mayhem landed," Deano noted. "That would be a juicy background angle to a story alright, but...Please, Henrietta, I have signed up Clo to play the *femme fatale* in my docudrama."

"Hmmm," the naive young reporter said, looking upward. "According to the TVC Academy press kit, someone fixed up this old hotel about ten years ago and put in modern windows that look like the originals, but don't open for anyone to jump or get pushed out of. That was one of the conditions for making it the headquarters for all the humbled-come-tumbledness-down temperamental TVC stars who won't win a Frito. So I don't see how Mr. Mayhem could have grabbed hold of..."

Windows that don't open? Damnit! Just like "fixed up" **Microsoft.**

"I can see how he did it, plain as a dropped egg on a plate of hash," said the more worldly mother. "Same way as Bill Shatner rescued his daughter from that no-account young tomcat who used **Priceline** to get a high-class hotel room for hanky panky: Bill put suction cups on his hands and feet; climbed up the outside wall; cut a hole in the hotel room window with a glass-cutter; and yanked out his daughter's fancy man. Romeo fell fifteen or twenty stories down into a swimming pool. In this case, it was no doubt that floozie her own self who cut open the hole and tried to pull the Mayhem character through it by his ears."

Deano rolled his eyes, but..."Except for the, uh, slightly overwrought suction cup bit, that would be quite an angle for a story set right here at the TVC Awards," he said. "You know: Life imitating spot art. But please, Henrietta..."

"Hmmm," the daughter again hmmed as she again looked upward, and then down at him. "I can't rightly tell from way down here, Mr. Deano, but when you were up in Ms. Clo's room this morning, was there a hole in the window?"

"Hmmm," Deano himself now hmmmed. "I didn't happen to notice, but now that you mention it, I now recall that I did feel a breeze. Of course any damage would have been repaired by now, but...Please, Henrietta, don't let your own mother's show biz career lead you to jump to any rash conclusions about what might have happened when Mayhem—a notorious masher—made unwanted advances toward Clo.

"And, uh, don't go up there to see for yourself right now," he added. "Clo is, uh, indisposed at the moment. But later…" Glass cutter? Deano again rolled his eyes. That bit too was slightly overwrought, but now it was part of the **Plan B** story he was stuck with.

SPOT #21

Stalking Miss Daisy

Though thankful to Mr. Deano for taking Wynona Sue off her hands—for lunch at a fancy restaurant and to tonight's TVC Hall of Fame induction banquet—Henrietta her own self was indisposed to getting het up about a story that his docudrama star, Ms. Clo, might have been responsible for Mr. Mayhem's fall. For her to report such a tale might look like she was giving in to her mother's nagging and promoting her to take Ms. Clo's place. Also, only a week ago, working for the Stockyards City branch of the OKC SCENE News Group, she had jumped like spit off a hot skillet to suspecting three different people of blame for causing a honky tonk angel's disappearance, only to find out it was a someone else who had pushed the gal into a hole that later got filled up with cement. Plus, during that filming of what was supposed to have been a pilot for a *Beauty Parlor Gossip* reality TV show—but turned into a "docudrama" about theft of women's underwear—Mr. Deano had already showed he was inclined to be scatterbrained.

And there was something out of plumb about the story he'd told but begged her not to put in the paper. After finding out that she her own self had not overheard Ms. Clo invite Mr. Mayhem up to her eleventh-floor room, the famous Hollywood producer/director had at least implied that his docudrama star resisted the overly romantically inclined **Allstate** Insurance TVC star's "unwanted advances." Based on her own experience with the "notorious masher," she could imagine him getting out onto that ledge to go a-courting, whether invited or not. And she supposed Ms. Clo might have changed her mind before he arrived. But until the **Transgressive** Insurance star got unindisposed enough for someone to come see if there was a repaired hole in the window of room eleven-o-seven, well, reckoning that she'd better get back to looking for ordinary news, Henrietta wandered up to the Grand Ballroom, where…

Huh, only two young fellas were there, setting at a table, with laptops open and staring at a big blank screen mounted to a wall.

"*SUPER BOWL: How the Commercials Won the Game* is being shown across the Media Center in the Centennial Ballroom," said the cute curly-haired one, who looked to be barely past his teenaged years. "All that's going on here is that Ethan and me got called in to edit some video that'll be featured at the big banquet tonight." In answer to her introducing—and inviting—her own self, he said, "Sure, hang out if you want to."

"The honchos want more nostalgia for all the old people who have showed up for the seventy-fifth anniversary of the spots art form," said the other one, Ethan, who was nerdy-looking and not so cute. "But there's not much vintage stuff to work with. The first ad agency bosses back then were too stupid to save the early time capsules that are part of the American narrative: More important signifiers of their times than great works of literature." The cute one laughed, said they were college film students and that his co-editor must have read that "pithy observation" in a Professor Hall's book. "Most early TVCs were focused on exploiting the hygienic, financial, sexual and intellectual insecurities of viewers," he his own self added, "and my name is Joel, by the way."

Oh, we're the men of ***Texaco****/ We work from Maine to Mexico*, sang a quartet of what looked like uniformed security guards that suddenly appeared on-screen. *Our show tonight is powerful/ We'll wow you with an hour full…*

The picture changed to show—also in black-and-white—two simple cartoon figures at a piano, singing ***Piels****,* ***Piels****, glorious* ***Piels****/ Glorious, glorious beer…*but Joel clicked a keyboard button that erased it. "The honchos don't want to show any animation," he explained. "They've decided to focus on individual characters who are, or were, played by live actors—including mainly those in long-running integrated campaigns who are called stars—which will be what this year's Frito Awards are all about." Another animated spot, advertising a brand of pesticide and titled *Garden*, showed some snails stalking a cluster of daisies-with-faces that were huddled in terror—which was kind of disturbing—and that one got edited out too. Then came what Ethan called "demo" spots, showing how products—including a watch that "kept on ticking"—worked under stressful conditions.

Followed by "time capsules" of baseball players eating **Wheaties**, "Breakfast of Champions," and smoking cigarettes; followed by lots of women keeping houses clean; followed by a flirtatious gal, and a man's voice-over asking: *Does she…or doesn't she?* Ethan said that after the **Clairol** hair coloring ad got aired in 1955 the number of American women who dyed their hair jumped from seven percent to fifty percent. Then came a barrage of sexy women: One, wrapped in feathers and laying on a big box of **Muriel** cigars, singing *Why don't you pick one up and smoke it sometime.* Next, a slinky gal in a tight dress got squeezed out of a giant tube of **Brylcreem** hair goo for men and asked, *Are you man enough to try it?* before planting a big wet kiss on his lips. A gal who looked and talked like she might be from somewhere overseas came on and told another male shaver to *Take it off, take it all off.* After an ad for a man's cologne—"**007**: License to kill…women"—another woman with an accent said, *When you use 007, be kind.* And then another good looking gal came on and said nothing got between her and her **Calvin**s.

"What the heck happened to chicks in the Sixties," Joel asked. What happened was that the birth control pill got popular, Henrietta happened to know; but didn't say for fear of sounding like his high school Biology teacher. As a bunch more spots played on the screen—now all in color and mostly musical—she got to thinking of the curly-haired college film student as almost her own age.

"Here's a classic we gotta keep," said Ethan, as a video clip showed a man flubbing shot after shot of him eating dinner, then trying to say the line: *Mama mia, that's a spicy meat-a-ball.* The spot seemed to be for a jar of **Magdanini**'s meatballs setting on the table, but no…"And this other **Alka-Seltzer** classic too," the nerdy film editor said, about an ad that showed another man who had obviously got overfed, saying: *I can't believe I ate the whole thing.*

"I wonder who this old actor was who played Colonel Sanders back then?"

"He's no actor, Joel. Colonel Sanders was a real person before he became a character, so this spot has to go."

"And this creepy old guy too, 'Mr. Wipple', who would be

arrested today if caught copping a squeeze of '**Charmin**' tissue paper at a supermarket."

You've come a long way, baby, said a voice about a woman smoking a cigarette, followed by a rough-and-tough looking cowboy, standing beside a horse, saying: *Big bubbles. No Trouble*, then blowing a big **Hubba Bubba Gum** bubble.

"Check out this metrosexual dude, Joel. Says here he was a famous football player named Joe Namath who didn't actually shave his legs and wear women's pantyhose as a rule. Yeah sure. Cut him."

A spot titled *Fast-Paced World* came on, but…What in tarnation? A character named Mr. Spleen talked so dern fast on a phone…*Dickit'sadorkwithDonDealandDave.Dave gottago. Davegottago, disconnecting.Dorkgottago,disconnecting.Dongottago, disconnectingDick*…she couldn't understand what he was advertising.

"That **FedEx** spot takes too much time, and we've just now got to the Nineties," said Ethan.

"And almost all the aught spots have been planted by the **Sonic** drive-in fast food chain," Joel added.

Both video editors leaned back in their chairs and sighed. "Well, we know we have to cut Mr. Mayhem and Flo off the back end," said Joel.

"And we know Shatner wouldn't sit still if we squeezed in any other stars of his era," said Ethan."

"Let's cut to the chase, use a clip of Shatner…"

"Delete a bunch of **Sonic** spots, and bring down the curtain."

But before we reach the ending may we add/ Remember to be loyal to our gasoline and oil/ When they save you time and toil, you'll be glad/ They're the best friends your car ever had.

"Okay, that's a wrap."

As the two college students went to working their keyboards, Henrietta wandered over to a stage, where a semi-familiar, though odd-looking fella with blue eyes and dark black hair—aided by an also oddish gal with spiked, bleached hair, plus an arm tattoo saying HOG WILD—were spreading a cloth on the head table.

From behind her own self, "Would you, um, wanna hang out after tonight's banquet," said the semi-whispered voice of Joel.

Henrietta turned around and saw he was blushing, as he went on and said: "I'm, um, living with my mom right now, just temporarily, but maybe we could go to your place and, you know, um, hang out."

Dang it, she had not, um, "hung out" with a fella since Gus was a pup, but realized that with Wynona Sue in town and no doubt wanting to stay with her at the Wobbly Boot Hotel, she her own self was in the same fix as Joel: Just temporarily living with her own mother. Feeling like a high school girl was worse than seeming like a high school teacher.

SPOT #22

Cloudy With Chance of Meatballs

After leaving Jimmy to soak in her YMWLGBTQ?CA room's bathtub, then getting into the Skirvin Hotel with Agent Clack's credentials and password, Shirley had easily blended in with the hotel's kitchen staff. A middle-aged bus boy, Enrique—as if sensing a kindred spirit—had been especially welcoming. Though he had strangely blue eyes, he was black-haired and obviously Hispanic; probably with I.D. documents, if any, as bogus as hers. While naturally inquisitive about where she was from, what prior work experience she had, etcetera, he was understandably evasive about his own background; revealing only a star-struck excitement to be serving *las estrellas de television* who had descended upon the hotel. In particular, the locally-based so-called **Sonic** Guys were not only *muy amusement* in his unsophisticated opinion, but also *los iconos perfectos para OKC*, his adopted American hometown.

She had volunteered to help set up the head table, but now that she was up on the Grand Ballroom stage and engaged in the task, it was hard to carry on without showing her true feelings. "By all rights, Jim…uh, Mr. Mayhem, should be up here tonight," she couldn't resist saying to her co-worker, "to receive the Lifetime Survivalship Frito."

"*Si*, he was quite a *hombre*," Enrique replied. "A TVC *estrella grande* and high roller, but a pigeon."

"Pigeon?"

"Gambler who chase his losses, and in *Señor* Mayhem's case, a mush."

"Mush?"

"Player who tilts the table, brings his run of bad luck to others."

"You talk as though you knew him, personally."

"Not *muy mucho*, but we happened to cross paths last night just before he…I can't help feeling *loco* for what happened."

"What did happen? Where and when did you cross paths? Why do you feel *loco*? Tell me, Enrique, *por favor*."

"Well, he stumble into kitchen from the alley, in a daze. Black eye, bloody nose, split lip, but sober and steady on his feet. He want to get to the eleventh floor in worst way, but say he couldn't risk being seen by someone who might be tailing him, so…"

"So?"

"So I led him up the fire stairs and…leave him there, standing next to an air vent. He must have got confused; thought the vent cover was door out to the hallway, and…well, *que sera, que sera*."

Shirley barely resisted an urge to plunge a butter knife into the chest of the negligent senior bus boy. But it wasn't really Enrique's fault, she then realized. That **Progressive** Insurance Company tramp, Flo, was to blame. Jimmy must have been trying to heist that damned price gun of hers. And besides, she needed to remain on duty—and on Enrique's good side—to have a chance of wreaking revenge.

She watched him like a hawk as he began to put place cards on the long head table. *Mr. So-and-So, one meatball*, was written on one card. *Ms. So-and-So, one meatless black bean ball*, said another. *Mr. Shatner, three jumbo meatballs & **Chef Boyardee** mini-bites version of **SpagettiOs**, with extra tomato sauce...Mr. So-and-So, one meatball...*

"I wonder which undeserving so-and-so will win the Lifetime Survivalship Frito now that Jimmy is out of the picture?" she asked.

Enrique looked up from his card-dealing with a quizzical expression in his blue eyes.

"I'm a member of a Mr. Mayhem fan club, 'The Mayhemettes'," she added. "Though none of us has ever had the privilege of meeting him in person, we think of *Señor* Mayhem as our 'Jimmy'."

"None of you 'has' had the privilege'?" he said. "You make it sound like the *hombre grande* is still...Anyway, all I *comprende* about tonight's Frito winner is that he, or she has acid reflux of the bowels and is to be served..." He shuffled through the place cards, and then said: "One-quarter meatball, no salt, no pepper, absolutely no spices or seasoning of any kind; and a side order of **Alka-Seltzer**."

"Gee, that could be almost anyone," Shirley said, before turning away and going about the business of putting silverware on the head table, while humming the tune of "Plop, plop/ Fizz, fizz/ Oh what a relief it is!"

SPOT #23

Oldest Trick in the Book

Henrietta wandered from the Grand Ballroom to a nearby Crystal Room, where the OKC Chamber of Commerce was hosting what was listed as a V.I.P. wine and cheese tasting party. A friendly gal handed her a glass of red wine and with a bright smile welcomed her to the event "catered by *En Croute*." She was feeling semi-peckish but three men in their senior years stood around a table, hogging a tray of cheese and crackers, real frugal slices of ham, plus an assortment of nuts and olives. As she circled them, looking for an opening to serve her own self, the stoutest one said, "You know, I was raised in this part of the country myself, and probably would still live here if a whirlwind had not whisked me up to Harvard with a crop of other burly hayseeds."

"Off to see the Wizard, huh, Willie?" said one of the others. "Landed a job on Madison Avenue and never clicked your heels to return until . . "

"Are we in Kansas?"

"Ol' Ozzie Cochran was in fact my boss at the time he got that 'wizard' reputation," said the Mr. Willie. "He convinced a **Prudential** Investments CEO to appear in some spots, looking like he actually had the brain, courage, and heart of a reasonably… And by the way, Wickie, that's what I like about the Fritos as compared to the damned Emmys: Honesty. Hell, television and the damned internet are not information media, and damn sure not entertainment media. They are goddamn advertising media, plain and simple. The only purpose of boob tubes and laptops is to provide a way to sell stuff. Period."

"Well, my work for the Academy would be for naught if it weren't for real Mad Men like you and Wally here," said the Mr. Wickie, as he put an arm on the shoulders of the third one, a baldheaded Mr. Wally, who seemed confused about where he was. "You fellas have unloaded a lotta stuff through the years, with both arms tied behind your backs. Not just limitations on airtime, but on content too. Hell, in the name of all that bullshit about free speech and art, you can show and say anything on television that the Devil could think of, and then some, but not in ads."

"I'll say," said Mr. Wally. "Networks show Jay Z and Beyonce practically doing the dirty deed on-stage, but turned down the spot of her promoting her perfume brand, **Heat**, just because it showed her long bare legs. To sneak anything sexy into a spot you've gotta be subtle."

"Yeah, like that **American Express** ad showing Tina Fey sitting on a yellow exercise ball," said Mr. Wickie; "telling a store clerk she used to have one, but with a face on it. Helluva kinky turn-on, but like you say, subtle."

"And yet they rejected my agency's trifecta spot for **Cialis** and the **Energizer** bunny—a freaking mechanical rabbit—okay, doing it to the **Chicken of the Sea** mermaid, but inside a gunny sack!"

"And last year the Better Business Bureau came out against that creepy Rob Lowe spot. Put the kibosh on **Direct TV**'s campaign for not being, quote, 'factual'. Better Business, my ass! Those bastards have started sounding like the Commies at PBS, who claim there's something more, quote, 'worthwhile' about programs that aren't paid for, except by **Uncle Sam**."

"They don't mind running vanity spots, saying sponsored by, say, the Otto and Dariel Stack Foundation."

"And don't forget their take from 'viewers like you', Willie. If I'm not mistaken, I think I even saw your's and the wife's names crawl across the bottom of the screen during the most recent month-long PBS begathon."

"That was Lola's doing, and the cheesy 'gift' she got in return for a two-hundred-forty dollar 'donation' was about what you used to get for sending in ten cereal box tops and a dime."

Ha, ha, ha…

Henrietta reached for an olive, but Mr. Willie got to it first. "Mark my words, boys," he said, after then finishing off a hunk of cheese that would have about filled a cereal box, "we're not in Kansas anymore. Trump's a meathead, in my book—nothing but cold-cuts for brains—but…"

"A helluva brander."

"…not George Soros. Hell, the son of a bitch broke the Bank of England. And now word on the street is that he's gonna make a play to take over MSNBC; get rid of all those hollow talking heads; sell airtime directly to **Move On-dot-Org**, **Black Lives Matter** and the like, 'stead of paying those high-priced shills to pass on canned sales pitches."

"Yeah, some Academy members wanted us to give a Frito to that Chris Matthews fella, but—just like Trump—it turns out he's a real buffoon, actually playing himself. We only recognize the legitimate characters you guys create."

Ha, ha, ha...

"Like I say, boys, Trump is a meathead, and we're not in Kansas anymore."

Reckoning that she her own self, as only a news reporter, should not be eating a nut off the V.I.P. tray anyway—or drinking red wine neither—Henrietta "clicked her heels" and went back to work.

In the Media Center, TV lights and cameras, plus a mob of reporters were re-assembled, including Ms. Peg Patterson from WOKC-TV, who had the baldheaded **Farmers** Insurance Guy backed up against a wall. "We know a thing or two because we've seen a thing or two," he was saying, as usual except for how loud he said it. "Four years ago a married couple residing in Richmond, Virginia, filed a claim for loss of their purebred English Bulldog named 'Spot'; supposedly killed in an accidental trash can fire. Our adjusters, however, noticed that the 'canine' remains tasted suspiciously like a **Smithfield** ham. Oldest trick in the book..."

"Are you telling my viewers that your adjusters tasted the remains of James Mayhem?"

"...sure enough, six months later, a strangely hairless bulldog named 'Baldy' won a blue ribbon at the Richmond Dog Show, but—under interrogation—answered to 'Spot'. So of course we didn't cover the so-called 'loss'."

"Are you telling my viewers your adjusters interrogated the remains of James Mayhem?"

Before the agitated **Farmers** Guy could answer, the Mayor again stood up at the podium and started talking: "Contrary to malicious rumors being spread in various quarters," he said, "mainly those of envious other cities not chosen to host this year's Frito Awards, the body of the dearly departed James Mayhem was not 'stolen' from right under my nose. I repeat: The body was not 'snatched'."

Ohhhhh…

"The truth is simple as a ham sandwich: James Mayhem's recently re-married mother, a Ms. Robin Click, showed up at our fine city's fine morgue; produced valid documents issued by the **Allstate** Insurance Company; and loaded the family remains into a nondescript **Chevy** van, as was her maternal right and responsibility."

Ohhhhh…

"So let's put these malicious rumors to rest and…"

"Are you telling my viewers the remains of James Mayhem tasted like a ham sandwich?"

"No, no, no. I'm just saying…"

Henrietta turned to the **Farmers** Insurance Guy—abandoned by Ms. Peg—for a comment. "Oldest trick in the book," he said, wiping his horn-rimmed glasses with a handkerchief, "including the Good Book: 'Mary the mother of James watched the Crucifixion from afar and later showed up at Jesus' tomb'. This is all 'crucifiction' made up to launch a new **Allstate** spots campaign."

"Are you saying the Mayor's statement about what Mr. Mayhem's mother did was made-up from out of a good book?"

"Yep. I am well acquainted with James Mayhem's **Allstate** family, and this latest stunt is typical of 'Mother'. Mark my words: Within the hour, rumors will spread that her TVC superstar is back on his feet. Within twenty-four hours, photo-shopped and dubbed spots will show him—a mischief maker turned repentant martyr—walking on water and spreading **Allstate** 'gospel' that anyone who puts their faith in so-called 'cut-rate companies' risks death and damnation. Mother is a Mad Woman who speaks with a forked tongue."

Land sakes alive. Henrietta reckoned any word of Mr. Mayhem's "second coming"—even if not true—would be sure to steal the show at the big Frito Awards finale scheduled for about twenty-four hours from now.

SPOT #24

Casting (Out) Calls

With her confidence in Marty Lowry's so-called **Plan B** waning by the minute, Chloe continued to lie on her hotel bed, watching the *E!* channel as Marty applied fresh putty around a window frame. Earlier, a butch-cut blonde *E News* reporter had repeatedly interrupted regular programing, each time with a new and different angle on "the suspicious disappearance" of James Mayhem's physical remains. Initially, the **Progressive** Insurance Company was suspected of snatching the body to hide evidence—such as "Pussy Galore's" fingerprints on his private parts—that *E News* naively thought the bosses "feared" would implicate Flo in the **Allstate** star's fall, which had been unbearably irritating. Then suspicion fell upon **Transgressive** Insurance, but only for supposedly trying to find or plant evidence: Such as traces of medications advertised as having side effects, including sleepiness, dizziness, fainting, jock itch, erections lasting longer than four months, depression and thoughts of suicide not covered by the "jumper's" **Transgressive** policy.

No mention whatsoever had been made of her, the **Transgressive** TVC star. And for the past hour media attention had refocused on living nominees for Fritos, such as the good looking young **Old Spice** Man, now on the TV screen—wearing only a towel—for "Celebrity Sit Down." *Look at me,* he said. *Now look at your man. Now back at me. Smell him. Now me. Smell the **Old Spice** "Swagger." And by the way, I have **Direct TV**. Don't you?*

Now look at me, said a far less attractive unclean-looking man sitting beside him—wearing a black motorcycle vest—*I like to smell armpits. I have cable and use **Manly Man** "Bear Glove" after-shave cologne.*

*We'll be back to sitting down with the **Old Spice** Man and Super Creepy Rob Lowe after this message from **Odor Eaters** for Women.*

When you yearn for your man to lick your feet...

BREAKING E NEWS! again came on the screen, then the face of that butch-cut blonde, who breathlessly reported:

E News has learned from multiple sources that there have been sightings of James Mayhem—alive and looking reasonably well—walking about Oklahoma City and spouting biblical proverbs. "Believe not what is said by an immoral woman," he is reported to have shouted, "for her lips are sweet as honey, and her mouth is smoother than oil. Beware of she who eats and wipes her mouth and says she's done nothing wrong." Most who are gathered here in OKC for the Fritos Awards believe he must have been talking about Flo. No one has a clue as to the identity of the woman he was thinking of when he went on to advise mankind to trust only "a repentant prostitute from whom seven inner demons have been cast out."

"Don't let that infotainment show spook you, Clo," Marty said from across the room, where he was now sprinkling bits of broken glass onto the carpet. "You yourself saw Mayhem fall from way up here," her agent needlessly reminded her, "and not even he could have survived mayhem like that."

Chloe wasn't "spooked," but in view of James Mayhem's budding *postmortem* status as at least biblical prophet and perhaps more, she now felt definitely disinclined draw attention to herself as possibly his, uh, Judas goat. Oklahoma City was a notch-hole in the Bible Belt, if not its buckle, and with rumors swirling…

Lending credibility to reports that ***Allstate****'s TVC star has indeed risen from the dead are rumors that the insurance company's ad agency is already working on a new campaign in which—who else but—the swashbuckling James Mayhem himself would star as "Jim Dandy to the Rescue."*

Chloe clicked-off the television. Back to a slightly modified version of her own Plan A: "Marty, I've made up my mind," she announced. "I will remain in seclusion tonight, but not to look 'suspiciously in hiding'. To the contrary, I absolutely forbid you and that other garden gnome to promote a story implying that I had anything to do with…with whatever happened to that man."

"But Chloe," said her agent, rushing to her bedside, "you promised Deano you would star in our docudrama as a hooker, and we're counting on you to come across as a *femme fatale.* A sensationalized scandal will enhance…"

"I shall play the role, brilliantly, but not as a villainess. I now see myself as a whore with a heart of gold, who—you know—does it for free."

"But Chloe, our sponsor is **Capital One** and the title…"

"Enough already, Marty. Clean up that mess you've made and fetch me a **Burger King** Whopper—extra pickles, hold the lettuce—with a double-order of **Sonic** Tater Tots and a large Slurp 'n' Burp. I am ravenous, and gaseous."

Chloe thought it highly unlikely that James Mayhem would

reappear in the flesh to star as "Jim Dandy to the Rescue" for **Allstate**. But she herself, after playing an adorkable whore in Deano De-Whatever's docudrama, would then be the perfect casting choice for the successor the dearly departed **Allstate star** himself had endorsed to carry forth his message: A trustworthy "repentant prostitute from whom seven inner demons have been cast out."

SPOT #25

Don't Eat That, Lady, It's Horseshit

Henrietta stood off to the side of the TVC Hall of Fame banquet. Ballroom lights dimmed. Music started playing. On the screen behind the elevated head table, a big circle appeared. Outlined in black, with lines coming out from the center, the circle looked sort of like a wagon wheel, but...*This is what was called a test pattern*, said a booming male voice. *At the time of television's creation, people stared at this image on tiny screens for hour upon hour in wonderment, not realizing it was in fact an ovum awaiting fertilization. Now watch. On July 1, 1941, a spark of life finds its mark, and voila!*...As lightning flashed and thunder clapped, the test pattern morphed into a watch face...*The first TVC is conceived in this ten-second spot for* ***Bulova*** *timepieces!* Black-and-white video next showed an egg getting lifted off a golf tee by a **Band-Aid** plastic strip, then lowered into a pot of boiling water. A voice said, *Plunk your magic twanger, Froggy!* and a rubber frog came on the screen. A dog barked. A young freckled-faced boy popped out of a shoe. *That's my dog, Tige*, he said, *he lives in a shoe. My name is Buster Brown, and I live in there too.*

The audience clapped and cheered like Okies who had seen pictures of a Donald Trump tweet.

After some spots she had already seen...*Then came the glorious years of the Fifties*, the narrator's voice-over continued, as clips of the quartet of singing security guards came on the screen. *TV shows were mostly live and the main ones, such as the* ***Texaco*** *Star Theatre, were produced and sponsored by a single advertiser; occasionally two or three, who often ran feature-length sixty-second ads, live!* Other film clips showed women making cakes and casseroles in kitchens, then one gal struggling and failing to open the door of a **Westinghouse** ice box she was advertising...A man admiring hisself in a mirror as he combed his hair and someone sang: ***Brylcreem****, a little dab'll do ya/* ***Brylcreem****, you'll look so debonair/* ***Brylcreem****, all the girls will pursue ya/ Try a little* ***Brylcreem*** *on your hair*...Then, a show title—*$64,000 Question*—came on, followed by video of a woman, identified by a caption as Dr. Joyce Brothers, scratching her head.

The banqueters booed and hooted like highly educated New Englanders who had seen pictures of a Donald Trump tweet.

Many Americans fretted about the future of television when advertiser sponsorship of programming became unaffordable for most companies, but not NBC's true believer, Sylvester Weaver. When he could not find a sponsor to foot the bill for Meet the Press, he—no doubt inspired by the famous loaves-and-fishes biblical lesson—said to his flock: 'Why not divide ad time into fifteen to thirty-second segments available not just to the few, but also to the many. Yes, Saint Sylvester was a prophet: After his epiphany, the American public started seeing spots!

Everyone got up, started clapping hands, stomping feet and chanting, *Hallelujah! Hallelujah! Hallelujah!* Dozens of TVC clips from the Sixties onward flashed on the screen, again including some she'd already seen, along with others she'd missed while flirting with Joel: A **Volkswagen** Beetle being drove through deep snow by a man going to work as a snowplow driver…A bunch of men dressed in white, standing in a U-shape like a mouthful of teeth, saying farewell to one named Harold—dressed in a brown outfit—who had to leave because he didn't use **Crest** toothpaste…Lots of happy young people drinking lots of **Coke** and **Pepsi**, while singing about how good the beverages made them feel…A Brother Dominic putting down a feathered quill pen, going to a **Xerox** machine to print five hundred copies of the bible overnight, and his boss at a monastery calling it a miracle…A one-second spot of a bullet hitting a **Master Lock**, but not breaking it…The famous pink **Energizer** bunny making fun of the claims of competitive TVCs by drumming his way through fake ads for phony products such as "**Airdale**" room freshener…Spot after spot of the **Sonic** Guys, setting in the front seat of a car…And finally…

Henrietta reckoned Wynona Sue must be downright swooning at the sight of her hero, William Shatner, appearing on the big screen as *THE NEGOTIATOR*…Picking up his baby-blue phone and saying, *I'm willing to do whatever, wherever, whenever, to save you up to fifty percent on car rentals, hotels and airfare. A steal, you say? No, that's negotiation. Name your own price with* ***Priceline…****But before we reach the ending may we add/ Remember to be loyal to our gasoline and oil/ When they save you time and toil, you'll be glad/ They're the best friend your car ever had…*The ballroom lights came on, and Mr. William Shatner his own self stood up at the head table. The crowd that had come to see an induction into the TVC Hall of Fame about went wild.

After taking a big gulp of something from a glass and letting the applause quiet down, "Hello, suckers!" the **Priceline** star bellowed. "And I'm not talking just about you dummies out there who booked your airfare, rental car and hotel by 'bidding' via **Travelocity.** I'm talking about you washed-up TVC actors out there who didn't have the cojones to name your own price for your services, like I did. Oh yeah, no toiling for minimum wage by Yours Truly, THE NEGOTIATOR. I busted a move on the **Priceline** suits and got stock options that are now worth a billion bucks!"

As the crowd cheered and Mr. Shatner took another gulp, Henrietta recalled reading that the famous negotiator had got a stake in the **Priceline** company when it was starting up, but after an internet bubble busted, sold his stock for a lot less than it was now worth. Still, even if he made only a million dollars…"I negotiated for my mother's breast and my first nippled bottle," he hollered, "and a playpen to boot. Mistakes? Maybe a few. But hell, I have sued myself, and won. Everyone needs a vacation, so of course I got fifty percent off a trip to a gulag in Siberia…" He took another gulp…"which reminds me: There are rumors going 'round that TVC fans are waging a write-in campaign for Donald Trump to get this year's Best Character Frito."

Some in the audience booed but most cheered.

"Puh-leeeze, gag me with a spoon. I have gone mano-a-mano with The Donald in dozens of negotiations and never ended up with less than fifty percent off his price. Most recently, I named my price for a luxurious Putin Suite at one of his hotels booked-up by the Denver Broncos for the night before a Super Bowl. In a nutshell, here's how the negotiation went:

"'No way,' the Trumpster said. 'Christie, Peyton Manning and I are bunking in Vladimir's digs.'

"'Have it your way,' said I, 'but if Manning loses sleep because of, say, a sudden invasion of bed bugs, and the Broncos lose . . .'

"'Okay, but only forty percent off.'

"'Sixty.'

"'Okay, sixty off, but no fruit basket.'

"'Throw in complimentary mini-bar privileges, a banana, and maybe…'

"'Sign a confidentiality agreement and you got a deal, Shatner,' he said. 'How would you like to run for Vice-President on my ticket?'

"Ha, you dummies want a wall along the Rio Grande? Elect me President. I'll give you a wall, make Mexico pay for it and take ninety-nine percent off every hotel room and rental car in Cancun for every hard working American, for life!"

SHATNER, SHATNER, HE'S OUR MAN…

As William Shatner emptied his glass, a man wearing a green plastic visor—the senior accountant who had presented the unimportant Fritos this morning—sidled up and handed him an envelope.

…**IF BILL CAN'T DO IT, NO ONE CAN!**

"Oh yeah, I almost forgot," said the famous TVC star, before ripping the envelope open. "The Frito for Lifetime Survivalship goes to…Mrs. Fletcher, former star of the **LifeCall** 'I've Fallen And Can't Get Up' campaign."

Mrs. Fletcher sped up next to Mr. Shatner in her wheelchair, rose up to reach for her corn cob statue and…Oh no, the Frito Award winner grabbed her belly, staggered, and…"I've been poisoned, and I can't throw up!" she hollered, before toppling across the head table and off the stage onto the ballroom floor.

Ohhhhhhhhhhhh…

The informally dressed **Farmers** Insurance Guy rushed to her, tried to lift her back to where she fell from, but…He dropped her, turned to the audience, and yelled that the hotel's insurance policy would not cover any claim for personal injury or head table damage resulting from "an obviously staged event."

Ohhhhhhhhhhhhh...

Henrietta ran over to poor old Mrs. Fletcher, got down on her knees and commenced to blow air up her nose. When she her own self rose up to catch a breath, the winner of the Lifetime Survivalship Frito looked up to her with watery eyes and commenced to mumble "**Al...ka...Selt...zer!**"

SATURDAY

SOMETIMES YOU FEEL LIKE A NUT

SPOT #26

We Are Farmers! Bum-Dadum-Dum

At a wee wee hour, Shirley lay in her bed at the YMWLGBTQ?-CA, wide awake and worried. Following last night's incident involving the **LifeCall** bitch, Mrs. Fletcher, law enforcement thugs had descended upon the Skirvin Hotel kitchen like fuzz from a copse of windblown Cottonwood trees. After hauling off **Chef Boyardee** and his assistants, they'd not even questioned the lowly staff about the alleged "poisoning." But they would be back for her today, she feared, rising from the bed. The time had come to make a run for the border. Careful not to make a sound, she crossed the darkened room. Inside the bathroom, with the door closed behind her, she switched on a light and…there lay Jimmy in the bathtub. A tube led from a now empty bowl on the floor to an opening in the cast that covered his head. She went to him and found that an eighteen-hour soak had reduced the plaster that encased his body to the spongy consistency of angel food cake dough. To her relief and delight, his hands….

Pardoneme, muchacha mio, but I have to relieve…" said a voice from behind her her. "Holy *burrito*! What's going on here?"

It was her co-worker—and overnight guest—Enrique, standing in the doorway with a startled look in his strangely blue Hispanic eyes. He, obviously an unAmerican 'Dreamer', had been as shaken as she by last night's invasion of cops, perhaps even more so. In a state of panic, not foreseeing his need to use the bathroom, she had offered him sanctuary.

"In the tub de bath…Is that…? Is that…? *Buenos dios*, is that the…the plastered TVC *estrella* I think it is?"

"Yes, it's Jimmy," she admitted to her *amigo*. "He's alive, thanks to his stout vital organs and that awning that broke his fall. He's started struggling to get his hands out of the cast and onto, well, let's just say I'm quite sure he must have that devilish look in his eyes and will soon be back to causing a certain kind of 'mayhem'. *Vamoose* with us, Enrique, I have a nondescript **Chevy** van parked in the alley, fully equipped with electronic devices and a ninety-day supply of food, water and ammo. *Ândele arribe* with us, now, without delay…"

"No, no, no, *muchacha mîo*," he said, backing away "Better to leave the *señor* in…in traction."

After going into the bedroom and talking things over, Enrique's advice began to make sense. Out of the cast, Jimmy might need medical care. A hospital and doctor would charge an arm and a leg. Better to get him out of the tub and go on as though nothing was amiss until nightfall, he counseled. With TVC stars clamoring for room service within the next few hours, *federales* would not dare hassle the remaining hotel kitchen staff. "You heard what that idiotic Mayor keeps saying," he pointed out. "The show must go on."

And her Hispanic friend proved to be right. After giving him a head start—and on second thought, loading Jimmy into the van just in case—when Shirley entered the hotel kitchen at dawn, Enrique and she, the only two staff members to show up, were treated like heroes by the hotel's ordinarily haughty Assistant Manager. As they together went about scrambling and plating this and that for the housekeeping crew to deliver to Mr. So-and-So in room six-seventeen…Ms. So-and-So in room nine-twenty…and to other early risers, Enrique began to softly sing: *Plop, plop, fizz, fizz/ oh what a relief it is…*She joined in: *Plop, plop, fizz, fizz…*

"Timely jingle," said someone from behind her. Startled, and frightened, Shirley turned to see that a bald man—wearing horn-rimmed glasses, a sport coat, tie and vest—was holding out a glass of water; addressing not her, but Enrique. "Where do you keep the **Alka-Seltzer**?" he asked.

Enrique went to a cabinet and opened a jar of the well known remedy for upset stomachs. The bald man plopped two tablets into the glass of water and…"Here, you drink this," he said to Enrique. "You look like you could use it."

Oh no. The deceptively friendly-seeming intruder was obviously a cop, Shirley thought, and obviously suspected that someone—namely Enrique—had served the **LifeCall** witch a glass of poisoned **Alka-Seltzer** last night.

Though looking terrified, Enrique gulped down the fizzy liquid.

"Good," said the cop. "I'll just hang around for awhile, to make sure you don't keel over. The hotel carries a **Farmers** policy, and we know a thing or two. Specifically, we know that **Life Alert** hired a TVC actor to fall down like Mrs. Fletcher used to do for **LifeCall**; added the word 'Help' to the line 'I've fallen', and deleted the words 'I can't get up' from the catchy slogan. So there's no telling how far their Mad Men might have gone to take that crotchety old woman out of the picture and have the spotlight focused only on their own wobbly star."

Enrique, though looking sickly after drinking the **Alka-Seltzer**, stayed on his feet, but Shirley was not the slightest bit relieved. The bald man—whom she now recognized as not a cop exactly, but the wily **Farmers** Insurance Guy—did in fact know a thing or two, she herself knew from her experience on the **Allstate** top secret Dirty Tricks Committee. Now he was over by a shelf of condiments, looking for another thing or two, humming the tune of "Plop, plop, fizz, fizz…"

Poor Enrique, now ashen, looked like he had in fact been poisoned. Fearful that he might blurt something about Jimmy, she went to her frightened Mexican co-worker's side and took his sweaty hand in hers. Shirley herself felt no pity, remorse or guilt about what happened to the wretched old woman who stole Jimmy's Frito, but what about Enrique? Would her undocumented *amigo* be blamed for what was God's righteous will?

"Hmmm," said the **Farmers** Guy, back to check on Enrique's condition by peering into his fear-struck blue eyes. "Have we crossed paths somewhere before *Señor*?" he then said. "I never forget a face."

SPOT #27

Curses! Foiled Again

Excited as all get out, Henrietta tiptoed to the door of her Wobbly Boot Hotel room and went out into the hallway. She'd told her mother in no uncertain terms to either drive on back to their little ol' hometown after last night's Hall of Fame banquet or get her own room if she stayed in OKC for the night, but…At the sight of Wynona Sue propped up in the double bed—with white **Olay** night cream all over her face—Joel, the cute curly-haired film student, had took off like a scalded cat. Only after gabbing at length about how she was "not at liberty" to tell how she got a "V.I.P. invitation" for tonight's Frito Awards ceremony—and her neediness for a new outfit—did her mother finally roll over and start snoring.

Henrietta her own self, on the other hand, had hardly slept a wink as she imagined presses rolling somewhere to print the big story she'd sent in to the OKC SCENE News Group boss man. She was right on top of poor old Mrs. Fletcher after she got dumped off the stage by the **Farmers** Guy, and the only one who heard what the victim said. A front page *OKC Tinseltown SCENE* article headlined **FRITO WINNER POISONED BY ALKA-SELTZER** might not be important enough to win one of those Pulitzer Prizes, but would likely keep her employed, she reckoned.

In a snack room downstairs, she got a cup of coffee out of a vending machine, a newspaper out of another, and without even setting down at a table…dang it!

AT&T GUYS CONFESS PLOT

by
Sylvia Bird

Questions about the suspicious presence of the ***AT&T*** *Guys at this year's Frito Awards in OKC were answered late last night following the TVC Hall of Fame induction banquet when the two characters—neither nominated for a Frito—confessed that their giant telecommunications company is plotting a hostile bid to take over the locally-based* **Sonic** *chain of drive-in restaurants. "Yes, we have been secretly studying the intercom system* **Sonic** *uses for fast communication with parked fast food customers," the smaller, darker-skinned* ***AT&T*** *Guy finally admitted to local police authorities after hours of interrogation. "Incorporation of* **Sonic** *technology into our network will absolutely wipe out competition from* **Verizon** *and* **Sprint***, plus result in faster fast food. It's a marriage made in heaven for both parties. Can we go now?"*

Sonic *issued a written statement strongly condemning an apparently coordinated attempt by the supposedly innocent* ***AT&T*** *Girl known as "Lily" to trick their TVC Guy into a shotgun marriage. "Lily is a gold-digging little whore and likely a foreigner, who recently said 'Opa! Welcome to my big fat Greek network' in a spot after* *snaring* ***Direct TV*** *in her spider's web," according to one high level* ***Sonic*** *official, who did not want to be identified, or quoted, for fear of stirring up more trouble for the ongoing TVC Awards festivities already beset with trouble: First, anonymous threats were made against Fritos contenders. Late Thursday night,* ***Allstate*** *Insurance Company TVC star, James Mayhem, fell from an eleventh-floor ledge of the Skirvin Hotel. Last night's TVC Hall of Fame induction ceremonies were marred by the apparent poisoning of* ***LifeCall****'s fallen but still beloved lady, Mrs. Fletcher.*

The Mayor expressed condolences to the entire ***LifeCall*** *family and ordered local flags to continue flying at half-mast, while firmly dismissing allegations by some that this is a minor league city. "Mrs. Fletcher met her fate, doing what she loved best," according to His Honor, "and would want the show to go on, regardless of collateral damage to some." Suggestions by concerned citizens that the Governor call out the National Guard…*

Henrietta couldn't read no more. Dang it, a Sylvia Bird, ordinarily just a reporter for the *WEEKLY Bricktown SCENE*, had got a byline for a front page story about the **AT&T** Guys that she her own self had set right on top of. In a semi-tizzy, she thumbed through the paper, searching for anything she her own self had sent in. Finally, on a back page, in a catch-all column titled ***Stars of Yesterday Sightings****: Robert Wrenn, 1971 Frito Winner for an* ***Odor Eater*** *spot, and according to Wikipedia,1968 nominee for another spot starring Oklahoma's own Mickey Mantle that brought chewing of* ***Brown Wad*** *tobacco from playing field into elegant New York City penthouses.*

Knowing that was not the level of journalism likely to impress the OKC SCENE News Group boss man enough to keep her employed—much less win one of those Pulitzer Prizes—Henrietta set down, opened her spiral notebook, and commenced to review leads about who might be a next victim.

The **Farmers** Guy? Hmmm. She'd got a notion he was not such a likable "good ol' boy" as he seemed in TV spots, bragging about how happy his company was to pay claims.

Colonel Sanders? Hmmm. From what she'd seen at the cocktail reception, those two black fellas didn't much cotton to him, and the **Transgressive** Insurance Gal, Ms. Clo, had slapped his face for some reason.

What about Ms. Clo? And her sister, Ms. Flo too? Hmmm.

The **Sonic** Guys were the most likely next targets, Henrietta reckoned. The Mayor obviously thought they were in danger, which was probably why neither one had been seen in public since the cocktail reception on Thursday. And though the **AT&T** Guys were likely either still in custody or run out of town by now, their company would likely still be trying to take over the **Sonic** network. If the **AT&T** Girl, Ms. Lily, was really the gold-digging spider she was said to be, and out to trick one or both **Sonic** Guys...

On the other hand, if all the mischief-making was intended to make OKC look unglamorous, the dirty deeds could be random, Henrietta reckoned. Any ol' TVC star could be next: The **National** Car Rental Guy...The ex-**Verizon** Guy who now worked for **Sprint**...the Most Interesting Man in the World... The **Burger King**...Even Ronald McDonald.

Hmmm.

SPOT #28

Yesterday the Pits, Today the Wrinkles

Deano stepped out of a Skirvin Hotel elevator on the eighth floor, dreading the early-morning command performance called for by the two Stans. He had been turned down by the black **Allstate** Guy and knew of no other African-American TVC star who might...At the sight of a hulking brown dude loitering in the hallway outside the Stanley & Stanford hospitality suite, he thought Lady Luck might have arrived in the nick of time. "Deano DeBoffo, famous Hollywood producer/ director," he said to the skinheaded bro, handing him a business card. "Are you, by any chance, a TVC actor?"

"Yeah, I am, and a good one," the guy said, taking the card, then producing a pen from a jacket pocket. "You want the autograph made out to your 'grandson', 'Little Deano', or just..."

"No, no, I'm not a fan...I mean I don't have any grandkids, but I might want your 'John Henry' on a contract to play a starring role in a docudrama I've got in the works. Interested?"

"Maybe," the guy said, handing back the autographed card.

"I ain't getting the love I deserve in my current gig. Are you invited to this evening's big-shot **Sonic** party?"

"No, but, see you there to seal the deal," said Deano, glancing at the card. This dude, "Charles Barkley," had a dumb look in the eyes that was perfect for a thuggish pimp, demanding to know: "What's in your wallet?"

Inside the hospitality suite, "Stan, my man, how they hangin'?" he said to Stanley. "Stan, my other man, how…?"

"A little tight," said Stanford. "Let's step into another room and review a few small details of your project, DeBoffo."

The creative Stan, seated across from him on another bed, said: "After sleeping on it, Stan and I…"

"…think that angry black Attorney General might file criminal charges for 'profiling' if we backed a docudrama along the lines you've suggested," said the other Stan, now seated beside his partner.

"You know, I've been thinking along the same different lines, Stans, my men," said Deano, with a sigh of relief. "Maybe a thuggish Latino or Asian…"

"Stan and I have been thinking along a slightly different different line, Deano. Have you seen that **Visa** spot featuring the young married couple? The guy is black, and an American Olympic champion. The female lead is a white Canadian, and also an Olympic star. So…"

"So we want you to dump the **Allstate** black guy, who is currently the subject of rumors that he had something to do with getting the other **Allstate** Guy, Mayhem, out of his career path to becoming a TVC headliner."

"…and use the famous ex-basketball player, Charles Barkley, who…"

"…we're already contracted to pay. He's…"

"…already associated with a **Capital One** campaign, but…"

"…a dumbass."

"…Jackson and Lee constantly make fun of him."

Though confused, Deano could hardly believe his own dumb luck. "No problemo," he said. "I just now saw your man, Barkley, out in the hallway, and thought what a perfect thug…"

"You're not listening, DeBoffo. Charles is dumb, but, uh…"

"…sensitive," said the creative Stan. "And well, we would like to see your docudrama move away from any sort of thuggish pimp-and-prostitute scenario to a more upbeat **Visa**-like love story."

Love story?

"Simple, DeBoffo. To get the ball rolling, you get Barkley down on his knees in Episode One, proposing to that other all-white insurance company broad. She coos something along the lines of 'Oh my', then pops the classic romantic question: 'What's in your wallet?"

Other insurance company broad?

"The **Transgressive** Insurance Girl—the one named Clo—is perfect for the role, Deano. More virginal than Jennifer Garner, in a weird sort of way. Never married, I'm told. Totally unscathed by scandal, unlike her sister—that **Progressive** bimbo you lined up—who seems to have been involved in something tawdry with the white **Allstate** Guy, Mayhem."

Ordinarily, Deano would have at least bridled at intrusion of business suits into his role as producer/ director—usually the effect was to shrivel plums into juiceless prunes, so to speak—but under current circumstances…"Great idea, fellas," he said, springing from the bed. "I'd better get right to lining up the other…You said Clo, the **Transgressive** Insurance broad, right?"

Silently cursing Marty Lowry—while muttering a hopeful prayer that the little strawberry blonde newspaper reporter had not taken the bait for an exposé about what happened inside or in the vicinity of room eleven-o-seven Thursday night—Deano hustled from the Stanley & Stanley suite, into the hallway and toward the elevator: Bound for the "scene of the crime" Marty had staged for that stupid **Plan B** of his.

SPOT #29

A Counter-Offer Dey Couldn't Refuse

Chloe again lay on her hotel bed, again watching *E!* network coverage of the build-up to tonight's Frito Awards, while yet again waiting on her agent to wait on her. As it turned out, Marty, though wrong in stubbornly counseling exploitation of her ill-fated dalliance with James Mayhem, had been dumb luckily right in advising her not to bother attending last night's Hall of Fame banquet; in both cases for the same reason: That wretched **LifeCare** woman's failure to make a graceful exit after too many years of milking bygone TVC celebrity had stole last night's spotlight, and at the same time pushed the whodunnit angle of the Mayhem story completely off-stage, so to speak. Sister Flo's fifteen seconds of *femme fatale* fame as a "Pussy Galore" had now passed from public consciousness like a so-called Public Service spot. Though there seemed to be some local gab about a petty personal rivalry between the **Sonic** Guys and **AT&T** Guys, national media was now focused on the more important matter of who would win the Best Female TVC Character Frito.

Golly, Ms. Flo has been my idol since I was a teenager, the sickeningly sweet **AT&T** Girl was now saying on "Celebrity Sit Down." *If it were up to me, she would have been awarded the Lifetime Survivalship Frito last night. Her large body of work through the years is almost as...Well, Flo has played such a big part in our industry for so long, I am honored to even be mentioned in the same category.*

"Large body" of work through the years since you were a teenager, Lily? said that skinny *Saturday Night Live* actress now known as the **American Express** Girl, who was also up for a Frito. "*You are such a phony little priss!*

*You're one to talk, Tina! In that stupid **American Express** spot showing you stocking up for a "cheese storm" at a supermarket check out line, you were obviously mocking big, fat Flo!*

*And I suppose I was bothering to mock sweet little you when I flirted with that guy across an airplane aisle in another **AmEx** spot. You are such a prick teaser!*

Girls! Girls! Please! Put away the daggers! There's been enough blood and bile spilled already, and the actual awards presentations won't take place—if ever—for another twelve hours. Let's all try to be...

BREAKING E NEWS! came on the screen, then the face of that butchy blonde reporter, again breathless.

*An elderly woman residing in Rancho del Vista, California, known to be the divorced-and-remarried mother of James Mayhem, has denied she is 'Robin Click'—the name of the woman who claimed her son's remains in Oklahoma City—and further claims that she herself would not be caught dead in a nondescript **Chevy** van such as the vehicle used by the body snatcher. Meanwhile, here in OKC, in response to an anonymous tip from a reliable source that James Mayhem is indeed up and about, E News staked out a police raid on the downtown Oklahoma City Y within the past hour. Our video* *footage was seized by the Chief himself, who had on his hands traces of what appeared to be either damp plaster or angel food cake dough. Stand by for more anonymous tips about what's cooking in OKC.*

KNOCK! KNOCK! KNOCK!

Chloe clicked-off the television and went to the door, irritated that it had taken so long for Marty to fetch…

"F.B.I." said a man, as he rudely barged into her hotel room. "Don't make a false move," said another ruffian who followed. "We would like to ask you a few questions about your actions late Thursday night," one of them said, as the other one began to paw through a drawer of her underwear. "There's no point in denying it, Ms. Courtney: We have surveillance evidence of you setting a honey trap for James Mayhem at the cocktail reception earlier that evening. The next morning we intercepted a call from Mayhem's controller—'M-O-T-H-E-R'—who last night sang like a strawberry blonde canary about how you attempted to 'entertain' the **Allstate** operative inside this very room."

"My mother is a notorious liar!" Chloe answered. "She always favored Flo, even before my devious sister sucked up to her by putting our entire redneck family in a series of **Progressive** holiday spots. No doubt James Mayhem, a complete stranger to me, was on his way to Flo's room down the hall when he fell from the ledge leading in that direction."

"You jealously intercepted him, right? Pulled him into this room of yours by his ears, right?"

"The windows in my cut-rate room don't even open."

"How do you explain the curious fact that no suction cups were found on Mayhem's crumpled body?"

Suction cups?

"No sign of them here," said the underwear rummager, "only falsies cups. And no glass cutter either, but…Hello, here's the pink lace nightie Mother told us about, with a piece chewed off the butt."

"My agent did that. He is...if nothing else, an exceptionally eager beaver."

"Funny that you ducked William Shatner's appearance at last night's Hall of Fame banquet. Why the no-show, Clo? Starting to feel the heat? Got cold feet?"

"Having myself decided to play the role of whore with a heart of gold, I didn't want to be seen in last night's circumstances as a *femme fatale*. My lousy agent..."

"Well, well, well, what have we got here?" said the G-man who had gone from pawing through drawers to..."Fresh putty around the window frame, and...What's this?" he said, stooping. "Looks like chips of broken glass from the window pane that was cut open and recently replaced."

"My agent is also a lousy housekeeper, so what?"

"So, to judge by the location and extent of damage to an awning down below, James Mayhem fell—or was pushed—from this very room, Ms. Cocker; that's what."

Overcome with sudden panic, "I wasn't here that night," Chloe cried. "There have been anonymous threats against me. My agent thought it best that I stay...Gentlemen, please, my clueless agent came up with the dumb idea of making it look like—just look like I'm an octopussy, but...Yes, my feet did get cold. I adore Bill Shatner, but didn't want to be seen in last night's circumstances as a...My producer/director, the short big cheese from Hollywood—Deano, uh, DeVito—used my ticket for **Plan B**, but I told my agent not to butter up a newspaper reporter and plant a story making it look like, just look like..."

"Mr. so-called 'Deano DeBoffo' may have had cosmetic surgery to make himself look like Danny DeVito, Ms. Courtney, but we're not fooled. Our agents spotted the Mafia *capo di tutti capo* for who he really is the minute he got off the plane from

Vegas. At last night's banquet, I myself noticed that he had a suspicious lack of appetite for **Chef Boyardee**'s meatballs before leaving the affair suspiciously early. And yet, soon as he got back to his room at the Y, guess what? Somebody holed up there took delivery of a pizza, from guess who? **Godfather's**. 'Da goods was in da box' alright. We found it this morning in the Y dumpster along with a few left-over anchovies; obviously part of a coded message to confirm that the mark, Mrs. Foster, was by then sleeping 'wit da fishes'. We've got **Chef Boyardee**—a/k/a Hector 'Mean Meatballs' Boiardi—in the cooker, but he's sticking to the *Cosa Nostra* oath of *omerta* and we're running out of time."

As the bust continued, Chloe began to get the picture and so did the federal fuzz: The *What's In Your Wallet?* "project" was a ruse the so-called Hollywood producer/ director had used to dupe her naive agent, and entangle her in his devious plot—under orders from unknown *Mafiosa*—to sabotage this year's Frito Awards. After learning from Marty that she had invited James Mayhem to her hotel room for the legitimate purpose of discussing a career alliance, the *capo di tutti frutti* had conned her and her pathetically gullible agent into trying to distract the G-men from their investigation: By dragging her like a red anchovy into a sensationalized story that she was a *femme fatale*. Both Feds truthfully admitted to now being less concerned about the fates of Mr. Mayhem and Mrs. Fletcher—that was cold pizza in their book—as they were worried about who DeBoffo was working for, and what he would do next to achieve his godfather's ultimate nefarious objective.

They offered to disentangle her, a mere pawn, so yes, in return for that—and their acceptance of her counter-offer they couldn't refuse—Chloe agreed to be a wired F.B.I. operative. Her assigned role—that of a "Pussy Galore" on the side of law and order—would allow her to display her acting talent and, finally, outshine Flo as a major star!

SPOT #30

Boomer Sooner!

By the time Henrietta got to the Skirvin Hotel another press conference was fixing to happen in the Media Center. Up at a podium, the Mayor took a gulp from a cup—advertising *SLURP 'N' BURP...This is how you* ***Sonic***—put down the billboard-size styrofoam container and commenced to talk:

"As Mayor, I am sorry to have to announce that, yet again, organized mischief has been afoot in this big league city," he announced, with a look on his face more feisty than sorrowful. "Thirty years ago, the **National Finals Rodeo** turned down our better deal and left us for the glitz of Las Vegas. Fifteen years ago, **United** Airlines rejected our better offer to subsidize a billion-dollar airplane maintenance plant, and went to Indianapolis. Ten years ago, Texican sumbitches down in Houston stole our homegrown **Kerr-McGee** oil company. The **United** Airlines folks later told us that the deciding factor that went against us in that case was that 'someone got to' the wives of their executives, and turned them against our local lifestyle for its alleged lack of fine restaurants and such. Well, by golly, now OKC is home base to the bigger-and-better **Sonic** chain of casual eateries, and we aim to defend our own from getting eloped-off-with by out-of-towners!

"I can understand how a company based in another city would be upset, even bitter, about the prospect of our hometown **Sonic** Guy winning the Best TVC Character Award," his Honor continued, with a burp. "Such an accolade would add immense prestige and value to the **Sonic** brand, making it much more difficult and expensive for anyone to, say, launch a hostile takeover bid. That's why—I'm just saying—such a company could be trying to disrupt this year's Frito Awards: To make our big league city look unglamorous to even the wives of local **Sonic** executives. If anyone out there thinks I am being paranoid, just ask yourselves: Would getting control of **LifeCall's** electronic monitor technology, in and of itself, justify poisoning its former TVC star? I'm just saying."

"What are you just saying, Mr. Mayor?" a reporter from out of town hollered. "Are you saddened for the entire **LifeCall** family, or sorry that the poisoning of Mrs. Fletcher makes this dirt-ball burg seem 'unglamorous'?"

"Are you just saying Mr. Mayhem's tumble was also caused by 'organized mischief'?" another one yelled. "Are other TVC stars at risk of falling victim to an unnamed company's 'terror campaign' against your big league city?"

"No, no, no, no, no," said the Mayor, holding out his open palms like he his own self was being attacked by terror. "There is no further risk whatsoever. In fact…this is, uh, Top Secret, but (Burp) off the record (Burp) I am pleased to announce that the Department of Homeland Security has finished its investigation and sent to the Justice Department's Anti-Trust Division a load of what I am sure will prove to be clear-cut evidence of below-the-belt attempts by a certain well known global telecommunications company to harm the glamorous image of this fine city. (Burp) Let this be a lesson to others: When confronted by outsiders, Okies stand together as one!"

"Does this mean your local **Sonic** Guys will come out of hiding?" a reporter shouted. "*E News* claims they have been cowering in fear?"

"Nothing could be farther from the truth," the Mayor sputtered. "Nothing exemplifies brave Okie solidarity better than Peter and T.J. **Sonic**, who are joined at the hip as though unseparated by birth; standing as one and utterly unafraid to face that little **AT&T** minx—and/or jealous male Frito rivals—mano-a-mano!" After taking another gulp of Slurp 'n' Burp, "Only out of an abundance of caution, has our fine Chief of Police—working hand-in-glove with the F.B.I.—ordered the Academy of Television Commercial Arts and Sciences to cancel all remaining official activities leading up tonight's red carpet event," his Honor announced, "and advised all TVC stars to stay out of the public eye and desist from reckless behavior until then."

Ohhhhhh…

"The day of the awards is always mainly about privately sponsored parties anyway," the Mayor continued. "I urge ordinary outsiders who are not invited to such bashes to visit our fine zoo, where the famously frisky and recently renamed 'Spotty the Leopard' is stuffed and on display in his natural habitat. Take an hour or two to gaze at the statue of a noble Native American atop the new dome of our fine state Capitol. Dine at several of the more than forty fine **Sonic** restaurants located within the OKC metropolitan area, where unlimited minutes of high-tech electrocommunication with the kitchen staffs are absolutely free. The show must—and shall—go on, but not until tonight's grande finale!"

Henrietta her own self had never seen the frisky leopard that briefly escaped from the OKC zoo decades ago, but had already looked up at the Capitol building's Indian statue from a distance, and ate her fill of hamburgers and hot dogs at a fine **Sonic** restaurant back in her little ol' hometown. Reckoning that news was not likely to occur at any such local attraction, she was thankful to not be an ordinary outsider not invited to the many parties that were scheduled to promote one thing or another. Maybe she would get lucky, and be on hand if and when something happened to a third TVC star at this evening's fancy **Sonic** cocktail buffet.

Inside the hotel coffee shop, she found Wynona Sue had in fact got hold of Fritos credentials and was now settled at a table, drinking coffee and reading the *OKC Tinseltown SCENE* article wrote by that other dang reporter. "Honey, you will never win either one of the 'ritzer' Prizes 'til you learn to write down on paper what people want to read," her mother said, putting down the newspaper. "That's what I did, and look where it's got me. I'm not at liberty to talk about it, but…You your own self already know what that **Transgressive** Insurance floozie was up to Thursday night, but didn't have the gumption to write about it, so I my own self…Anyway, I can't be seen on that red carpet in the Cinderella wedding dress I wore to the Hall of Fame," Wynona Sue then said, like she'd said about a hundred times last night in bed, "because, well, I am not at liberty to say more, but I am sure to steal the spotlight from a certain low-class insurance company TVC star," she now added for the first time.

After her mother went off to shop for a new outfit, Henrietta went to thinking about what the Mayor had said about organized mischief aimed at making Oklahoma City look unglamorous. According to what she'd read somewhere, the root of most conspiracy theories was a tendency to think of misfortune to one person, or place, as having been caused by some other person, or place, that coincidentally happened to benefit from it. And no doubt OKC had seen a lot of troubles through the years. Being located on the Plains, smack dab in the middle of Tornado Alley, there was always the weather to contend with. Local folks still talked about a Great Depression back in what were called Dust Bowl Days—wrote about in a famous book titled *Grapes of Wrath*—when Mother Nature forced poor Okies to pack up and head for California to pick crops when jobs dried up and the state's good dirt got blowed all the way to New York City. According to a TV documentary she'd seen awhile back—titled *The BOOM The BUST The BOMB,* made by an ex-Mayor—more hardship had been visited upon the city off and on in more recent decades, lots of it at least partly by the hand of outsiders.

Though Oklahoma City was born poor on left-over land not assigned to nobody—its only known resources being the grit of the people who moved in—later discovery of oil brought booms of prosperity, always followed by devastating busts. About the biggest boom was in the 1970s, when overseas events made the price of oil go sky high. Partly also because of economic hardship in other parts of the country at the time, a big bank up in Chicago threw their's and other big city banks' money into wind sweeping down the Plain to Oklahoma. And a little ol' local bank in a suburban shopping center called Penn Square dished it out to Okies who thought oil prices would never go down. Folks were so optimistic about the future they tore down more than half of downtown in order to build it back to something better. There was even a famous commercial on local TV that said, "If you don't have an oil well, get one."

Then came a big bust. Way more money had been loaned than what the oil wells got to be worth. So the federal government shut down the Penn Square Bank, and about everything came a-cropper. People lost their jobs and couldn't pay their mortgages, a hundred state banks had to close 'cause big out of town outfits didn't want anything more to do with Oklahoma, and about half of downtown OKC became a weedy vacant lot. That was at about the same the **National Finals Rodeo** relocated to Las Vegas, Henrietta recalled the documentary movie saying, and not long before **United Airlines** wives turned up their noses at OKC. But the Mayor back at that time was stubborn as a hair stuck in a biscuit. He got folks to vote for new taxes to pay for civic improvements—to invest in their own selves when nobody else would—in order to improve the quality of life for their kids and grandkids.

Then came the bomb.

That was when that Mayor back then and the people of Oklahoma City showed their true grit. They bowed their necks and kept on keeping on to the point that now OKC had a river with plenty of water in it and a canal that made a scenic setting for restaurants in the Bricktown entertainment district; a sports arena and a major league professional basketball team; big new buildings downtown, which had only one hotel at the city's low point but now had about twenty. So it was understandable, Henrietta reckoned, that the current Mayor would be proud, but at the same time sound maybe a little afflicted by what was called "paranoia": A mental condition of thinking someone was out to get you.

And like someone sorta said, just because you were paranoid didn't necessarily mean someone was not out to make your hometown look unglamorous

SPOT #31

Please Don't Seize the Charm-ed Pot

Alone in the Skirvin Hotel kitchen, Shirley stood at a hot stove, stirring a large pot of grease, mumbling: "Double, double, toil and trouble; fire burn and cauldron bubble." Had she a toad handy, or root of hemlock, or gall of a goat, she would have thrown it into the steaming kettle of gravy. High-and-mighty big shots, including the Mayor and Chief of Police, were upstairs; partying in the fancy so-called Venetian Room; thinking only of themselves. Though forewarned that unnamed TVC stars—possibly including Jimmy—were in danger if they dared to show up for the Fritos Awards, they had left the eleventh-floor ledge unpatroled on Thursday night. For their own privileged safety, however—and that of their precious locally-based **Sonic** Guys—the Police Department now manned all elevators and stairs, allowing only invited V.I.P. guests and select media to have access to the private wing-ding on the hotel's top floor. Since the gala affair was being hosted by **Sonic**, the fast food chain was catering the cocktail buffet.

"Slivered in the moon's eclipse, nose of Turk and Tartar's lips," she mumbled.

But the Venetian Room kitchen facilities, except for microwave ovens, were out of commission for some reason, and without a topping of hot gravy **Sonic's** signature Tater Tots were virtually inedible. Enrique and she—both eager to demonstrate good law-abiding citizenship—had agreed to tend to the menial chore of supplying the greasy topping.

"Double, double, toil and trouble; fire burn and cauldron bubble. For the ingredients of our cauldron..."

Uh oh.

The nosy **Farmers** Insurance Guy—though obviously disappointed that Enrique survived a dose of the kitchen's supply of **Alka-Seltzer**—had seemed satisfied this morning, but now he was back.

"Where is your Latino friend, Enrique?" he asked. Before she could answer..."I just left the Intensive Care Unit at Saint Anthony's Hospital," he said, wiping steam off his horn-rimmed glasses with a handkerchief. "Mrs. Fletcher is still in critical condition, unable to sign a routine form releasing the hotel and **Farmers** from any liability. But a Doc Shapard assured me that her gums are in good shape, considering her age; and confirmed that, technically, she was not poisoned."

Shirley gritted her teeth and continued to stir the gravy.

"The bad news, for her, is that the large amount of **Tabasco** sauce she ingested could still prove fatal, due to a clearly pre-existing acid reflux condition. After her bowels were pumped, our own adjusters identified the culprit: That was one spicy meat-a-ball!"

Shirley stiffened. Earlier, the **Farmers** Guy had nosed

around a condiments shelf, previously stocked with two large bottles of **Tabasco** sauce.

"We know a thing or two, 'cause we've seen a thing or two," he continued, but I have to admit: I can't believe she ate one-quarter of the whole thing."

Though tempted to explain the current absence of **Tabasco** sauce from the shelf—the entirely Hispanic kitchen staff poured the spicy condiment on all their free meals—Shirley continued to silently stir.

"I need to see the Mayor and the Chief of Police without delay, but…What's cooking?" asked the baldheaded snoop, bending over the cauldron, sniffing. "I was told the kitchen was to be shut down for the evening."

"Just gravy," she answered, "for the V.I.P. **Sonic** party."

"**Sonic** party? That event is being held in the private banquet room on the top floor. The Mayor and Chief of Police are up there and not even I was allowed…"

Buzzzzzzzz…

"Hello, what's this?" the insufferably persnickety TVC pitch man asked as he went toward a wall-mounted flashing red light: Enrique's signal that Tater Tots were to be served upstairs in fifteen minutes. "Well, I'll be a monkey's uncle," he said, after sliding open the door to a dumbwaiter and sticking his bald head inside.

"Toad, that under cold stone sweltered sleeping got/ boil thou first in the charm-ed pot."

SPOT #32

When E. F. Button Listens, People Talk

Deano sat at a corner table in the Skirvin Hotel bar, nursing an **Alka-Seltzer** on the rocks and stewing. After being dealt a new hand by Stanley & Stanford this morning, he had found the eleventh floor of the hotel sealed off by G-men. Possibly they were busting the other doll—"Flo," the **Progressive** Insurance so-called Girl —not "Clo"—the **Transgressive** Insurance so-called Girl—but he had a bad feeling in his gut that the story he himself had planted about the so-called *femme fatale* occupying room eleven-o-seven had blown up in his face. Damnit, the two Stans now wanted a "**Visa**-like" story line for the *What's In Your Wallet?* docudrama, starring a TVC actress more virginal than Jennifer Garner, and other than Clo—in their opinion—he doubted such a woman existed. Marty Lowry was responsible for the fiasco; both for suggesting they go for cheap, sensational publicity and by not babysitting his star. The so-called agent—probably wasting time with his other client, that local book writer—had not been reachable for hours; and when he finally did call back, seemed not worried that the Feds might frog-march their leading lady through the hotel lobby at any moment.

"No need to hit the panic button," he'd said on the phone, cool as a Santa Monica breeze. "Probably the G-men are just now picking up on the 'Pussy Galore' publicity about Flo. But even if they do talk to Clo, don't worry about her playing the role of *femme fatale,* because she now…I'll worm my way onto the eleventh floor just in case and meet you later in the bar to explain." Deano looked at his watch. Damnit, now it was hours past later, and…

"I've got good news and bad news," said the agent, suddenly beside him. "Let's have a beer and figure out our next move."

Uh oh, bad news, right on cue.

"The good news is that the strawberry blonde newspaper reporter never showed up to check the window in Clo's room…."

"So?"

"…so the fuzz didn't have any reason to even knock on Clo's door. She's been laying low all day, watching the *E!* Channel."

Though somewhat relieved, Deano took another belt of **Alka-Seltzer** and braced himself for the bad news.

"The only problem is that, well, Clo is, uh, temperamental; and now set on playing the *What The Hell Is That In Your Pocket* role as a sort of saintly hooker with a heart of gold. Don't worry, Deano, she'll come around. In fact, she's going to join us in a few minutes; says she wants to get to know you better before sealing the deal. So you can sweet talk her…"

Though embarrassingly short of walking-around cash, Deano waved to the bartender and ordered **Heinekens** for both of them.

"No problemo, Marty, my man," he said, with a slap on the agent's back. "By coincidence, I have been thinking about changing the docudrama concept—still titled *What's In Your Wallet?*—to a **Visa**-like love story."

"Love story?"

After walking the agent/ screenwriter through a sensitive black dude's marriage proposal to Clo in Episode One…"Deano, my man, you are a freaking genius," Marty said, "but…Where does it go from there? Where's the tension, the conflict, the drama?"

Obviously Marty had never been married. All wives started out as whores with hearts of gold, he explained, but morphed into black-hearted gold-diggers after a honeymoon phase ended midway through an Episode Two. "Believe me, Marty," he said, "wedlock is a lot more 'dramatic' than getting mugged by Samuel L. Jackson."

"The **Capital One** movie star?" said Clo, as she joined them. "Yes, he would be an acceptable co-star, but before we seal the deal, Mr. 'DeBoffo'—just as a formality—I want to know all about you. For instance…"

In answer to her question, "Yeah, married and divorced four times," Deano said. "Currently single, and intend to keep it that way."

"Four divorces?" she said, fiddling with a blouse button. "Like swimming with loan sharks, huh?"

"Yeah, dames go for the big vig, and then some."

"What were the reasons for the splits?"

"The usual: Incompatibility, mental cruelty, taller men with more hair."

"Hmmm," she hmmed, while continuing to fidget with the button.

"Before you ask, Clo, I admit: I'm currently a **Geico** man, but hey, what's fifteen percent when a guy's got 'Murphy' breathing down his neck? I'll sign up with **Transgressive** first thing tomorrow."

"'Murphy'? An Irish cop? Yeah, **Transgressive** policies are tailored for guys like you with records long as…longer than your arm."

Record? "Oh, you mean driving record? Over-parking at meters, wrong turns…?"

"Ever use an alias, such as, say, Capone, Luciano, Gotti, Soprano, DeVito?"

Uh oh, the Fritos Awards credentials in his wallet were in the name of Danny DeVito. Better to come clean. "Actually, my real name is 'Cosmo Magdanini'—born in Brooklyn—but you know how it is in Hollywood: All about glamorous image."

"'Magdanini'? Sounds like that might be a Sicilian name, right? You must be *paisans* with **Chef Boyardee** a/k/a Hector 'Mean Meatballs' Boiardi, who somehow got hired by the Skirvin Hotel for the Fritos?"

"The real Chef B has been pushin' up daisies for years. The guy they brought in for the Fritos must be a nephew or somethin', carrying on the family racket. Me, I make my own mean meatballs with mama mia's secret recipe?"

"'**Mama Mia**, that also sounds like a Sicilian brand. Extra spicy, I'll bet, and with lots of anchovies, right?"

"Like I say, the recipe is a Magdanini *famiglia* secret. I've sworn an oath of *omerta*, ha, ha."

As Clo continued to salt-and-pepper him with questions, Deano began to think of her as not exactly attractive, but kinda cute in a somewhat virginal way. Ordinarily even wannabe female stars talked only about themselves. So yeah, he had broken one or two of the Ten Commandments, he admitted. Once stole, well, he only took another kid's bike for a joyride.

No, he had not confessed any more recent sins to a priest but would tend to the oversight immediately, if not sooner. Sure, she was welcome to get in the booth with him. No, there had not been anything "personal" between him and a Mrs. Foster, the so-called **LifeCall** Lady who got "bumped off" at last night's Hall of Fame banquet, and he had no "vendettas" against—didn't even know—any other TVC stars.

"Spots are not really my bag," he said. "I mean, sure, fifteen to thirty-second segments are okay as promos for real screen dramas. And yeah, lots of young, up-and-coming stars—such as yourself, Clo—have used spots as stepping stones to Hollywood: Meg Ryan and Ben Affleck for **Burger King**. DeCaprio for **Bubble Yum**. Pitt for **Pringles**. Travolta for **Safeguard** soap. Jodie Foster for **Coppertone**, the Lohan bimbo for **Jell-O**, and in a Megan Mullally spot for **McDonald's**, John Goodman made a non-speaking debut before switching to **Burger Kin**g. But to me spots are too short to be an art form. Sure, for some wiseguys it's just business: You know, bim-bam-thank-you-ma'am, but as for myself..."

Deano, actually enjoying himself, waved for a round of drinks, plus a snack.

"True talent behind the camera, and in front, needs at least eight hours to dramatize the human condition through personal character development," he then continued. "Say the plot involves bumping off someone: You need to portray the victim as sympathetic and/or provide the doer with credible motive, preferably without distracting commercial breaks. I'm only attending the Fritos Awards in this dusty bowl of bad luck because I needed to...Well, meeting you, Clo, was a spot of good luck, but soon as I button up some unfinished business tonight..."

"You yourself are a button man?"

"...I'm getting' out of Dodge on a non-stop flight back to LAX."

"Los Angeles? I thought I heard someone say you flew in from Las Vegas."

As Clo continued to probe, Deano began to get an uneasy feeling that his docudrama star would not be satisfied that she'd gotten to know him unless and until he violated the oath of *omerta* he had sworn at his dying mama mia's bedside.

SPOT #33

Play the Dum Dums Lollipop Drop Game

Feeling like what her mother would call a "wallflower" at a fancy **Sonic** cocktail buffet party—happening inside what was said to be a Venetian Room that didn't actually have blinds on any window—Henrietta reckoned that by first thing Monday morning she would be permanently out of a job with the OKC SCENE News Group. The Mayor and Chief of Police seemed happy to talk to that reporter assigned from the *WEEKLY Bricktown SCENE*—Sylvia Bird—but had turned their backs when she her own self tried to ask if they knew of any new information about what happened to poor old Mrs. Fletcher. Other backs of people that circled around the **Progressive** Insurance gal, Ms. Flo, kept her from asking the famous TVC star about family relations with her sister, Clo. And another gaggle of reporters and fans had made it impossible for her to get a good gander at the famous **Travelocity** garden gnome. The only thing she had jotted in her spiral notebook was a quote from Captain Obvious that, while close to being true, was not fit for local publication:

"They call Oklahoma the Sooner State," he'd said, "because its college football team always exits the play-offs sooner rather than later." Absence of the **Sonic** Guys from the party in their honor was curious, but not newsworthy.

Reckoning she might as well leave the party, Henrietta started across the big room topped by a decorated curved ceiling and…"Hell's bells," Colonel Sanders said in a loud voice, "these **Sonic** Tater Tots are dry as yesterday's biscuits."

Both the Mayor and Chief of Police turned their heads and glared, first at the Colonel, then at the oddish-looking but semi-familiar black-haired waiter she'd seen setting up the head table for last night's Hall of Fame banquet—now dressed up in a tuxedo—who was standing next to a door of what looked to be a built-in cabinet. Wondering where they might have crossed paths before, she went on over to chat, but…

"Sorry, can't *hablo* at the *momento*," he said. "The dumbwaiter is on its way from the kitchen with a *mucho grande* kettle of gravy and I need to tend to it while it's hot."

A dumb waiter?

"We're shorthanded," he said, as a buzzer inside the built-in cabinet buzzed. "*Aquí* it comes." The Hispanic kettle tender, who seemed smart enough his own self, opened the cabinet door and stuck his head inside. After a few seconds…"Uh oh," he said, "something has gone *loco*."

Henrietta stuck her own head into the wall opening just as lights in the shaft went out, but saw, sure enough, elevator cables.

Buzz! Buzz! Buzz! Buzz!

All of a sudden, the cables started jerking back and forth as well as up and down, like the kettle of hot gravy must have took to lurching this way and that on its way up. Sparks commenced to fly off them down at what looked to be about two or three floors below.

"**Help! Help!**" someone down there hollered. "**I have seen a thing or two and now know a thing or two about who is responsible for**..."

Buzz! Buzz! Buzz!

The cables stopped jerking and..."**Help me, I'm fall**llllinnnggg..."

Land sales alive. Henrietta reckoned the **Farmers** Guy must have hitched a ride with the big kettle of hot gravy, to come up and tell the Chief of Police who was responsible for poisoning poor old Mrs. Fletcher.

"Please, everyone, stay calm and carry on," the Mayor shouted.

"Everything is under control," the Chief of Police added.

"Okies are accustomed to doing without gravy. So let's party on!"

Despite what they said—and despite the no doubt at least near fatal condition of the **Farmers** Guy—Henrietta couldn't ward off a thought that, dang it, she'd again barely missed getting a big story about troubles afflicting this year's Frito Awards.

SPOT #34

The Gospel According to Nielsen

With her undercover assignment for the F.B.I. completed, Chloe took her leave of Cosmo Magdanini a/k/a Deano DeBoffo. Since arriving in Oklahoma City on Thursday, she had not set foot outside the Skirvin Hotel and now it was Saturday evening. She longed for a breath of fresh air, and to be seen. But it wouldn't be safe for her to take a walk outside, Marty insisted. Fans of James Mayhem had reportedly gathered for a vigil of sorts. They might mistake her for her twin sister and—at the sight of the wrong "Pussy Galore" gadding about—might become enraged at the *femme fatale* they believed had brought down their hero.

Hmmm. That settled it. As she adjusted the blue headband of her costume that exactly matched that of the better known so-called **Progressive** Insurance star, "No, please, no," Marty begged. "Let's not do anything that might upset the apple cart."

"If they mistake me for Flo, why should I care?" she answered. "I might reveal her lack of remorse by mooning them."

"It could be dangerous, Chloe," whined little Marty, tagging along beside her. "How would you feel if the person you held responsible for harming a loved one…?"

"Exactly," she answered, though unable to think of a loved one off hand. "As for any danger, I feel certain I will be watched over by, uh, especially protective law enforcement personnel."

With Marty covering her rear, so to speak, she passed through the lobby and out the front door. An oval rotary serving the hotel entrance was blocked off, but across the way a mob of gawkers were gathered on the other side of wood barricades. "**There she is!**" someone shouted through a bullhorn. "**It's her! It's Flo!**"

FLO! FLO! FLO! the crowd chanted. **FLO! FLO! FLO!…**

Only when she drew nearer did Chloe notice that the throng of mostly women wore beaming smiles on their faces, some were in tears, and many carried signs mounted on sticks:

WE LOVE YOU, FLO!

HE HAD IT COMING, FLO!

WE'RE WITH YOU, FLO!

GO WITH THE FLO!

GO WITH THE FLO!

GO WITH THE FLO!

Obviously they were not enraged James Mayhem fans, but rather…Even better, Chloe thought, as she maliciously grinned and shot Flo's adoring flock the finger, with each hand.

Ha, ha, ha, ha, ha, ha, ha…

"That's our Flo!"

Ha, ha, ha, ha, ha, ha, ha…

"You go, Girl!"

Ha, ha, ha, ha, ha, ha…

Though she had been speaking figuratively to Marty about mooning Mayhem mourners, she turned her back to the mob, dropped trou and bent over.

"**That's not our Flo!**" the fan club pep leader bellowed. **"That's big, fat Clo!"**

BOOOOOOOOOOOOO…

Anti-Flo signs in remembrance of James Mayhem began to filter into the crowd:

FLO'S A FLOOSIE!

FRITO FOR JAMES!

NO FRITO FOR FLO!

FRITO FOR JAMES!

GO TO HELL, FLO!

Followers of the fallen **Allstate** hero chanted **DEATH TO FLO! DEATH TO FLO! DEATH TO FLO!**

Scuffling broke out. Someone threw a brick in her direction. But no one from the F.B.I. came to her side to provide the witness protection promised, and Marty seemed to have abandoned her. As she turned to flee, a gray-haired man climbed over a barricade, carrying a ***DEATH TO FLO!*** sign on a stick with one hand and what appeared to be a piece of lead pipe in the other. As he rushed at her, she saw a crazed look in his eyes.

"Please," she cried as he got in her face, "I am not Flo. I am the lesser star, big fat Clo! Didn't you see…"

"You are an immoral woman with lips sweet as honey," he viciously shouted, "and mouth smooth as oil!"

"No, please, it's Flo who eats, wipes her mouth, and says she's done nothing wrong. I am a repentant prostitute with a heart of gold."

"These writings say it is your kind who are responsible for my miserable life!" he ranted, while shaking a fist that held…not a lead pipe, thankfully, but rather what appeared to be a rolled-up magazine. "According to Nielsen, during the past sixty years I have watched five hours of television a day, including at least an hour and a half of commercials," he ranted. "That amounts to at least one hundred thousand damned spots that have both driven me crazy and wasted the equivalent of more than eight hundred forty-hour work weeks. You and your kind have ruined my life."

"No, please, I've only appeared in off hours, such as Sunday mornings."

"I could have played hundreds more rounds of golf!" the madman ranted, raising the sign above his head, the pointed tip of its stick aimed at her heart. "You must be stopped!"

As Chloe's knees began to buckle, a mounted policeman—with Marty on the horse also—clomped to her side. "Grab hold of the tail," her agent yelled, "and hold on tight!"

BOOOOOOOOOOOOOOOOOOOOOO...

SPOT #35

Out Damn Spots!

"Out of an abundance of caution," no one except the odd-looking waiter had been allowed to leave the Venetian Room until things had settled downstairs. So while people at the **Sonic** cocktail buffet—except for Colonel Sanders—went ahead and enjoyed their dryish Tater Tots, Henrietta had no choice but to cool her heels until…"Did you see or hear anything when you looked down into that shaft?" said that reporter assigned from the *WEEKLY Bricktown SCENE*—Sylvia Bird—suddenly standing there with pad and pencil in hand. Right beside her stood the Mayor his own self, who said: "I have already given Ms. Bird my eye-witness report and would like for you to confirm…" He turned his head to Ms. Bird and said, "tell her what the Chief said, Sylvia." Her OKC SCENE News Group teammate, looked at her notes, cleared her throat and reported: "Headline, 'Kitchen Kaper Kaput'. All evidence suggests that a brazen but futile act of vandalism by an embittered TVC star—likely acting on behalf of a certain global communications company—was intended to inflict a greasy spot on OKC's glamorous reputation.

Thanks to quick thinking on the part of a Skirvin Hotel staff member, the mischief maker was thwarted before..."

Act of vandalism? By the **Farmers** Guy?

"When you looked down there, did you hear him say anything like 'OKC SUCKS!'?" Sylvia Bird asked. "I'll be sure to give you credit, for a quote."

Reckoning that the poor old baldheaded **Farmers** Guy had got on top of the dumbwaiter to come tell the Mayor and Chief of Police something he'd found out about the poisoning of the poor old **LifeCall** gal, Henrietta told what she'd heard him holler: "'I have seen a thing or two and now know a thing or two about who is responsible for...Help me, I'm fallllinnnngggg...' "

"Hmmm," said the Mayor. "I hate to second-guess myself and the Chief, Sylvia, but I happen to know the **Farmer**'s Guy has been investigating the poisoning of that old woman on his own. Probably he only wanted to inform me that he'd found evidence to prove exactly what I have suspected all along."

Dang it, though knowing she should feel more dreadful about what happened to the tediously inclined **Farmer**'s Guy, Henrietta couldn't help being just as upset by the sight of Sylvia Bird now jotting a different story—no doubt quoting what His Honor had said—that was mainly based on what she her own self had seen, heard and partially suspected. The Mayor—who hisself had seemed more worried about the loss of gravy—looked at his watch, smiled with a look of satisfaction and, finally, announced that everyone was free to go down to the Fritos Awards ceremonies, scheduled to start in fifteen minutes.

After hightailing down fire stairs and exiting out the backside of the hotel...Land sakes alive! Thousands of people were coming down Broadway Avenue like tumbleweeds blowed by a fierce windstorm; lots of them carrying neatly printed signs—most saying either ***OKC IS BIG LEAGUE!*** or ***OUT DAMN SPOTS!***—and chanting one thing or another:

The show must go on!
Out damn spots!
Hell, no, Flo's a ho!
We want weed!
Goods are bad!
Occupy Madison Avenue!
Out damn spots!
Free TV for all!
Feel the Bern!
Bern down Wall Street!
Down with capitalism!
Down with consumerism!
Down with greed!
Out damn spots!
Make America great again!
OKC is big league!

Barricades put up earlier were now manned by armed National Guard soldiers. Military tanks were parked on each side of a long red carpet—lined with tall artificial palm trees in big pots and huge spotlights pointed up into the sky—leading from Broadway Avenue to a grand entrance to the second floor Grand Ballroom.

Less is more!
Spots are plots!
Only black lives matter!
Feel the Bern!
Down with white privilege!
OKC is big league!
Make America great again!

Henrietta went on over to a longhaired youngish fella holding up a ***KREDIT KARDS KILL*** placard and asked what exactly had him so agitated.

"Everything!" he hollered. "Gender-based rest rooms, putting criminals in prison, racial profiling, hot weather and everything else caused by capitalism . . ."

Let my people pee!

Lock up guns, not shooters!

White lives don't matter!

There is no Planet B!

"...especially television commercial spots," the youngish protester continued, "which are the means of production of stuff that no one needs."

Out damn spots!

Stop buying crap!

Buy less, work less!

Resist the buyological urge!

"...sugary breakfast cereals and soft drinks, faster and greasier fast food that also makes kids obese, more and bigger SUVs that spew CO2, and plastic..."

Feed the children!

Don't eat animals!

Fossil fuels for fossil fools!

No more credit!

No more spots!

"Consumerism is the bitter harvest, capitalism is it's seed, and advertising the manure that makes it grow."

Jingles drive you crazy!

Logos make you loco!

Don't get hooked on spots!

Just say NO!

Uh oh. Over at the grand ballroom entrance, the stout V.I.P named Mr. Willie—who she'd overheard at the wine and cheese tasting party put on by the Chamber of Commerce—threw a cigarette onto the sidewalk and came barreling toward her and the longhaired protester.

"You…you…you little spot of sperm! You should have been washed out with **Shiney Vaginey**," he bellowed at the youngish fella, "before you…you…you…grew up to be a Commie! "

"MAD MAN! MAD MAN! I'm being attacked over here by a Mad Man!"

"You're damn right I'm a Mad Man, and proud of it. If it weren't for TVC Guys like me, you wouldn't be wearing those four-hundred-dollar **NIKE** *Jordans*, those **Tommy Hilfiger** jeans, that **Under Armor** tank top, that ragged **Fred Perry** denim jacket, those **J. Crew** shades; and wouldn't have the credit card that paid your way here from…where? San Francisco?"

"MAD MAN! MAD MAN! Spying on us! Trying to wash our brains with TVCs!"

"I wouldn't waste a two-second spot or thimble of **Clorox** washing your brain, you…you…you freaking moron. Don't you realize you have forfeited whatever gray matter you were born with to the internet? **Google** does what passes for your thinking and you don't even know it! They transmit the data to us and… Hell, I could get you to charge a gas guzzling used **Hummer** to your daddy's 'kredit kard' if I branded it *ORGANIC*. Your, let me guess…Your **Apple** iMac, right? It has your puny brain stored in an infinitesimal bit of…."

"MAD MAN! MAD MAN! Now he's attacking **Apple**!"

Death to Mad Men!

Death to spots!

Death to…

BOOM!

At the sound of cannon fire, the mob of protesters scattered. Henrietta glanced at her watch, then ran down the red carpet. Climbing a grand staircase, she heard someone inside the Grand Ballroom holler through a loudspeaker: "**Let's get this show on the road!**"

SPOT #36

But Wait, Order Now, Get A 3rd Grab Bag At No Extra Charge

"You heard him sing the theme song for the **Mad Men** episode titled *Stranger in the Night*. You saw him croon to the **AFLAC** duck in the even stranger spot titled *What Happens In Vegas Stays In Vegas*. Now please welcome tonight's emcee, in person, Mr. Las Vegas himself, Waynnne Newton!" Though not a big fan of the casino showroom heartthrob of old bags dating back to the Fifties, Deano politely clapped his hands, while visually searching the crowded ballroom for Marty Lowry.

"*Danke schoen*," the Fritos emcee said, which also got a round of applause for some reason.

Though he had schmoozed Clo for more than an hour in the hotel bar—and sprung for a **Diet Pepsi** with **Cheez-Its** on the side—she had turned down his suggestion that they drop in on the **Sonic** cocktail buffet to meet her docudrama co-star: That dumb but sensitive guy, Barkley. And five minutes ago, seated at a table with five or six suits, she had given him a shoulder that would have chilled an Eskimo. No doubt the suits were

Transgressive Insurance big shots. Under the circumstances, she probably felt awkward, but…

"Ladies, please, this is not Vegas, sad to say, and I simply do not have enough time tonight to give your tokens of affection the attention I would like. Stop throwing panties at me!"

Ha, ha, ha . . .

Deano had never before seen Clo—nor any other TVC character—wearing ordinary clothes. For her to appear in public, out of her all-white **Transgressive** outfit and half into a revealing red dress—looking not exactly virginal—struck him as somehow ominous.

"Spots are like songs and performing in TVCs is a lot like singing," the still famous casino crooner continued. "Both are about how the words and performer make the audience feel, which is what we most vividly remember. And I can tell you this: All the nominees for Best Female Character make me feel like the hot-to-trot teenager I still am in appearance!"

Ha, ha, ha…

"The **American Express** Girl, Tina, sure gets my humorous bone to stand up and take notice in this one, titled *In Your Face*," Newton said, as video on a screen behind him showed a skinny dark-haired babe bouncing up and down on a big yellow ball.

Rah, rah, rah…

"And how about the **AT&T** girl next door, Lily, shown here in a spot about…"

BOOOOOOOOOOOOOOOOOOOOOOOOOOO OOOOO . .

"…which goes to show: You don't have to take it all off, ladies. Teasing is pleasing."

BOOOOOOOOOOOOOOOOOOOOOOOOOOO OOOOO…

"Clo's in an industrial-grade snit," said Marty, after coming up beside him. "She stepped outside after we left you in the bar, and her sister's fans gave her a rough time. Those F.B.I. agents at her table have put her under 'round-the-clock witness protection, but…"

F.B.I. agents?

"…if Sister Flo wins another Frito, well, look out for a shitstorm, Deano."

Mr. Vegas walked the audience through a couple of other spot performances by other nominated female TVC stars, but then…"And what would a TVC Awards ceremony be without a nominated performance by our Flo," he said, as video of Clo's dead-ringer sister—riding with a motorcycle gang—played on the screen.

BOOOOOOOOOOOOOOOOOOOOOOOOOOOOOOOOO…

Jezebel!

Whore!

Murderess!

A guy wearing a green eyeshade came on-stage and handed Newton an envelope. An odd-looking dark-haired guy wearing a tuxedo stood by, with a golden ear of corn in hand. The emcee opened the envelope and…looked back at the visored guy, who threw up his hands.

Boooooooooooooooooooooo…

"The Academy Board has elected to make a last-minute Public Service nomination for an eleventh-hour performance, titled *The Bagmen Cometh*, that just now arrived by special courier," Newton said to a TV camera, as another spot began to roll behind him.

Uh oh. Deano saw himself on-screen, sitting next to Clo at

a table in the Skirvin Hotel bar. He heard himself say: *My real name is "Cosmo Magdanini"—born in Brooklyn—but you know how it is in Hollywood: All about the…oath of omerta…Yeah, I've broken one or two of the Ten Commandments, but…nothing personal between me and the* ***LifeCall*** *broad…*

Boooooooooooooo…

…plot involves bumping off someone. You know, bim-bam-thank-you-ma'am…just business…Soon as I button up a few things tonight…

You yourself are a button man? said Clo, fiddling with a button on her starched white blouse.

…I'm getting out of this dust bowl of bad luck on a non-stop flight back to LAX.

Los Angeles? I thought I heard someone say you flew in from Vegas.

Yeah, well, I'm a little under-staffed at the moment and didn't get the heads-up. Not 'til I made the scene in Vegas did I find out the locals here in Yokelville had pulled the red carpet out from under Sin City.

Booooooooooooo…

You must have been plenty pissed off.

You don't know the half of it. See, only about a month ago I made the mistake of trying to do a job in this red dirt region of nowhere, and have had bad luck ever since.

Boooooooooooooooo…

I'll bet your Sicilian buddies in Vegas are pissed off too.

Hell yes, they're pissed. Bruno Giordano's Ristorante Famiglia was counting on a big score this weekend. Now my man Bruno is stuck with, pardon my French, a shitload of ***Chef Boyardee*** *meatballs—overcooking in an un-airconditioned desert warehouse—with no guarantee he'll be able to unload the dried-out balls at a Fritos wing-ding out there next year. By then…*

Boooooooooooooooooooooooooooooo…

...they'll be even more inedible than the Chef B balls they served at last night's banquet.

Boooooooooooooooooooooooooooooooooooooooo...

So what did you do afterward, Cosmo; make a call to ***Godfather's*** *to order a...?*

No way. The 'godfathers' called me, to set up an early morning face-to-face about, uh, a change of plan.

Godfathers? As in "they"?

Stanley and Stanford. They call the shots. Me...To tell the truth, Clo, when push comes to shove in this racket, even a famous Hollywood producer/ director like me has gotta take orders delivered by the big bosses.

Boooooooooooooooooooooooooooooooooooooooooooo oooooooooo...

Oh shit. Two of the suits rushed from Clo's table to the Stanley & Stanford table, put gunny sacks over the heads of the two Stans, and...The next thing Deano knew, it was also burlap curtains for him. And the crowd loved it.

Rah, rah, rah, rah, rah, rah, rah...

"Winner of this year's Frito for Best Female Character in a TVC is that super-talented **Transgressive** Insurance star, Clo, for her performance in *The Bagmen Cometh*, produced and directed by the F.B.I."

HURRAH FOR CLO! HURRAH FOR CLO! HURRAH FOR CLO!...

SPOT #37

Arby's: We Have the Meats!

Land sakes alive. Deano DeBoffo a/k/a Cosmo Magdanini, a "button man" taking orders from godfathers? Henrietta could not have been more surprised. Her mother had been right, at first, not to trust the little runt, though wrong in changing her opinion of the famous Hollywood producer/ director when he hinted that she might get to replace Ms. Clo in a docudrama.

Wynona Sue, now standing beside her on an edge of the grand hotel ballroom—outfitted in white pants, apron and blue headband—could be none too happy that a "certain low-class insurance company TVC star" had not let her "steal the spotlight." Sure enough: "She's a no account floozie who doesn't deserve the attention," her mother opined. "But like they say, even a foul breeze across an overflowing cesspool will blow good odor in somebody's direction." She went on to explain that the "foul breeze"—Ms. Clo winning a Frito—meant the TVC star would no doubt go on to be in the movies, like Meg Ryan did, which would open up the role of **Transgressive** Insurance Girl to her, Wynona Sue her own self.

"The F.B.I. men thought I was a secret **Allstate** Insurance agent known as 'Mother', and promised they would see to it I got an audition in return for me telling how James Mayhem got up onto that ledge and what that floozie her own self was up to. I reckon she got out of the fix, and then some, as pay-off for tricking that no-account Cosmo Magdanini to spill the beans about what he and the **Godfather's** pizza bosses think about having the Fritos in Oklahoma City.

"You should have gone up there to that room eleven-o-seven and grilled her your own self, Henrietta. You were setting right on top of the big story."

Reckoning that her mother was again probably about right, Henrietta scanned the ballroom, wondering what other big story she might be setting right on top of.

The two **Sonic** Guys were back in public view, setting side by side at a table—even closer together than in spots showing them in the front seat of a car parked at a fine drive-in restaurant—and seemed to be getting along like honeymooners in a single bed. So dang it, there would likely not be a story of any size about any fireworks between...What in tarnation! TVC stars were known to get facelifts and the like to make theirselves look better for thirty-second appearances on-camera, or even gain weight on purpose to play a role. Still, it was strange to see that the two **Sonic** Guys had got up and were walking in the direction of a men's room—both in the same three-legged set of trousers—like they now really were joined at the hip like the Mayor said.

The two **AT&T** Guys were not likely to make another local appearance, she reckoned, and—dang it again—she saw no sign of any other TVC star rivalries likely to break out into violence. Henrietta felt a little pang—along with disappointment—about

Mr. Mayhem not being around to cause newsworthy…mayhem. And about that poor old crotchety gal, Mrs. Foster, also being waylaid. The **Farmers** Guy would likely have been stirring things up, if able, but for some reason she didn't detect a pang about his absence. Since the strangely youthful-looking Mr. Las Vegas had gone off-stage—back to his dressing room for a botox refreshment, she reckoned—there was no one up there except for that also odd-looking waiter, who was polishing the two gold ears of corn that were yet to be handed out for Best Male Character and Best Spot. On the big screen, current ordinary TVCs were being showed one after the other for entertainment of those in attendance and what was said to be a TV audience of hundreds of millions of people around the world, but…

Though the current commercial break was supposed to last two hours, Mr. Las Vegas came back on-stage and started talking:

"Welcome back," he said into a camera. "Nielsen tells us that you people out in TV land are tuning out and I have personal information that Donald Trump is getting antsy."

Booooo….

"I know, I know; some liberal airheads think The Donald is a meathead, but…"

Rahhhh…

"…we're longtime buds, and believe me: His head is packed with plenty of gray matter."

Rahhhhhhhhh…

"I personally know many reasons Mr. Trump will be a great president. He's already been where the other candidate would like to be: Riding on his own plane. Not having to worry about what hotels he stays in or how his family gets to Hawaii. So forth and so on. In addition, he's is a ratings magnet; and the

Academy has previously recognized most of what he's said in the current campaign as spots. So it's a win-win situation. Let's postpone award of the Best Male Character Frito—Donald is unfairly not eligible—and move on to awarding a Frito for Best TVC!"

Hurrraaahhhhhh . . .

"The nominees are:

"*I'm Just Sayin*". A documentary spot about an opposing presidential candidate's father who helped Oswald kill Kennedy, produced and directed by Donald Trump."

Hurrah!

"*Big Hands For The Little Ladies*. A presidential debate spot in response to personally insulting charges by an opponent, produced and directed by Donald Trump."

Hurrah!

"*Would Anyone Vote For That?* A gratuitous comment about an opposing female candidate's face, produced and directed by Donald Trump."

Hurrah!

"*Crooked Hillary*. Another brief documentary spot about another female political adversary."

Boooooooooooooooooooooooooooo...

"*Locker Room Talk*. A brilliant discourse on the prerogatives of male TVC stars, produced and directed by..."

Rahhhhhhhhhhhhhhhhhhh...

Land sales alive. As Wayne Newton went on naming spots by Mr. Trump, Henrietta reckoned that the presidential candidate—though said to be unpopular in Hollywood and New York City—was bound to...

"And the winner is," Mr. Las Vegas bellowed, "*I've Got All The Words!* Biographical spot, produced and directed by—who else but—Donald J. Trump, next President of the United States!"

Rah! Rah! Rah! Rah! Rah! Rah! Rah!...

"We'll be right back with presentation of the Best Male Character Frito after these brief two hours of commercial messages. So stay tuned."

While reckoning she should be thankful that no more harm had come to any TVC star, Henrietta continued to fret about not having come up with any exclusive big story for the *OKC Tinseltown SCENE* that would keep her employed. And the show was almost over.

SPOT #38

Now, All Together: Happy Anniversary to Spots

Shirley could have fled hours ago, either before or after explaining to police that because the hotel's regular elevators were sealed off, the **Farmers** Guy had forced his way onto the dumbwaiter. Possibly he had intended to assault a rival TVC star or stars—most likely the **Sonic** Guys—with the steaming cauldron of hot gravy, she'd suggested, which sent the coppers chasing after the ambulance that carried him away. No doubt because the fuzz was distracted, neither she nor her friend, Enrique—who had aborted the gravy delivery from his post inside the top-floor Venetian Room—were suspected of attempting to blot OKC's image. So she had remained in the kitchen, to clean up the mess, and...Jimmy had never been even nominated for a real Frito that truly recognized his talent. Ever the proud one, he had never actually attended the gala ceremony honoring undeserving others. So she had felt compelled to stay, and do what she was sure the big lug would have wanted to do in response to the lifetime snub: Cause mayhem, like him.

Enrique saw her standing in a wing of the Grand ballroom stage; came to her side, and said: "*Buenos dios*, what are you doing here, *muchacha*?!"

"I just had to be here for Jimmy," she explained to her *amigo*. "I felt I should…"

"Where is *Señor* Jimmy?" he asked, looking left and right. *Buenos dios*, *muchacha*, you should have made a run for the border. For you to be here tonight is too dangerous…for me!"

"Don't worry, Enrique, I would never tell anyone about you leading Jimmy up the fire stairs to the eleventh floor. You meant no harm."

"Yes, but…but people will know I befriended you," he said, while continuing to look left and right. "With all these *loco* Trump people around here, I could be…"

"You yourself have not raped or killed anybody, Enrique," she said, trying to calm his understandable fears of deportation. "And neither have I. On the radio just now, I heard that both that **LifeCall** witch and that **Farmers** Insurance doofus are expected to survive their mishaps, as has Jimmy, thank God."

"Where is the big lug?" her friend again asked, this time staring directly at her. "If the *federales* get their hands on him, he might blame…me!"

"Jimmy is tucked away," Shirley answered. "Better that you not know the particulars, *amigo mia*, just in case the *federales* got their hands on you. For your own sake…"

"Enrique!" someone shouted. "Get a move on! It's showtime!"

As Enrique returned to tending to the last remaining Frito statuette and the emcee from Las Vegas returned to the spotlight, Shirley stood firm in the wings—tending to a large cake set on a rolling table—waiting for the right moment.

"Okay, let's wrap-up this party with award of a Frito for Best Male Character in a TVC," said the mummified casino celebrity's lips, that along with his eyes seemed to be the only still movable parts of his face. "The nominees are…"

Oh for crying out loud! Video on a large screen showed three men, apparently naked, sitting in a bathtub.

"…all three co-stars—or should I say, tri-stars—for their coordinated performances in this trifecta spot, titled *Rub-A-Dub-Dub*."

Try my new Saturday Night Fifty-Dollar Family Tub, said old Colonel Sanders, *but don't touch your feet before you eat, and don't wash your hands 'til you've licked your fingers!*

Look at them, now look at me, back at them, now back at me, said the young **Old Spice** Guy. *They'll never look like me, but could smell like me if they added "Lionpride" body wash to the Saturday Night Family Tub.*

I'm the Creepy Rob Lowe, said the creepy Rob Lowe. *I don't have* ***Direct TV****, so I have to sit in the Colonel's Family Tub of grease to watch Saturday Night Live.*

Boooooooooooooooooooooooooo…

"Though he may be outnumbered and out-talked, don't rule out our next nominee. For his performance in *I'm A Travelin' Man*, the beloved…" Shirley fumed at the injustice of it all, as another creepy character—with not even lips moving—appeared on the screen: **Travelocity**'s totally uncharismatic garden gnome, who couldn't hold a candle to Jimmy Mayhem when it came to making an audience laugh, cry or moan.

Boooooooooooooooooooooooooo…

"Lest anyone say the Fritos are 'whitewashed'—like other awards I could mention—the Academy Board mandates that a nomination be made annually for performance by a smart black guy living next door to a dumb white guy. This year's nominee in this always inspirational category of spot is the black **Esurance** Guy, for his delivery of a double-whammy in *Out of Touch White Dad*.

The spot showed a white guy filling an above-ground swimming pool with a garden hose while looking at his phone and saying he'd asked his daughter to tell him how to save fifteen percent on car insurance in fifteen minutes. A black guy across a picket fence in the background shook his head with undisguised loathing and grunted, to as much as say, *what a dumb (bleep)!*

The phone signaled receipt of a text message and the white guy said, *IDK? What does that mean?*

I don't know, said the black neighbor with a disgusted smirk, before turning and walking away.

Loll?

Booooooooooooooooooooooooooo...

"While there's been a lot of gossip lately about bitter rivalries among TVC stars, our next two nominees have put at least one such rumor to rest by electing to join forces, names and bodies, to qualify for singular fame, fortune and friendship as collectively the Best Male Character: The-one-and-only T. Peter J. **Sonic** for..."

Rah! Rah! Rah! Rah! Rah! Rah! Rah! Rah! Rah! Rah! Rah! Rah! Rah! Rah! Rah! Rah! Rah! Rah! Rah! Rah!...

"Hold your applause, please, hold your applause. We're coming up on our closing forty-five minute commercial finale and..."

Rah! Rah! Rah! Rah! Rah! Rah! Rah! Rah! Rah! Rah!...

Shirley, furious, gripped the edge of the rolling table in preparation for making her move. Finally, the rah-rah-rahing died out.

"Now let's have a very, very brief moment of silence in fond remembrance of two beloved fallen stars—James Mayhem, the careless **Allstate** Guy, and Professor Burke, better known as the, uh, persistent **Farmers** Guy—to whom the Academy Board has granted honorary nominations."

Ohhhhhhhhhhhhhhhhhhh...

Honorary! Shirley was more embittered than appeased by the empty gesture.

"The Frito for Best Male Character in a TVC goes to...James Mayhem, the **Allstate** Guy!

BOOOOOOOOOOOOOOOOOOOOOOOOOOOOOOOO...

"Accepting the award in Mr. Mayhem's absence is his brother in good arms and hands, fellow **Allstate** star, soon to appear as 'Jim Dandy to the Rescue'..."

Beside herself with rage—only slightly tinged with vengeful gratification that Jimmy had finally won a Frito—Shirley pushed the rolling table bearing the large cake to the center of the stage.

"Cake?" said Mr. Las Vegas, obviously confused. "Nobody said anything to me about cake."

"Later! *muchacha*," Enrique hissed, as he stepped forward with Jimmy's polished Frito in hand. "We'll all sing 'Happy Anniversary to Spots' after..."

Shirley reached beneath the table and pulled a lever, propelling Jimmy's doughy upper body out of the cake into an upright position. Another jerk on the lever raised his arm above his head, with stiff middle finger upraised higher.

OHHHHHHHHHHHHHHHHHHHHHHHHHHH...

As Enrique took it upon himself to present the golden ear of corn, the celebrity emcee tried to physically restrain him. "No, no, no, you fool," he said, "he's in no condition to accept the corn cob and will only drop it. Can't you see the man's had some work done recently!"

After struggling to get the Frito from Enrique's grasp, the so-called "Mister Vegas" looked into a TV camera and bellowed: "On a final happy note, I am pleased—and relieved, as I'm sure everyone will be—to announce that the Academy Board has unanimously decided that next year the Frito Awards will return..."

PFFT!

SUNDAY

SOUR GRAPES OF WRATH

SPOT #39

What Happens in OKC Sometimes Stays in OKC

Henrietta charged a refundable airplane ticket to her **MasterCard**, got through the airport security detectors and went on down a long deserted concourse. At Gate 8 she set down in a waiting area and began to re-read the final edition of the *OKC Tinseltown SCENE*:

FRITOS FIASCO!

by

Sylvia Bird

OKC's hosting of the Fritos Awards ended not with a bang but a fiery fizzle last night when the TVC Academy announced that beginning next year it will return forever to its ancestral home at the Wonderland Hotel & Casino in Las Vegas, come hell or no water. "Good riddance," said the Mayor immediately afterward; still visibly angry that a Frito statuette loaded with gunpowder semi blew up, ironically, in the face of the event's emcee known as Mr. Las Vegas.

"Obviously our **Sonic** *Guy should have received the award," his Honor added, "but this slap in the face in no way makes our big league city look unglamorous. To the contrary, the snub serves only to cinch the Justice Department's case against a certain global telecommunications company and its partner in crime, the Mafia. We had already decided not to again roll out our fine red carpet for future Fritos Awards anyway. So there, OKC is the true winner!"*

Henrietta looked up from reading and, sure enough, along came none other than that odd-looking waiter, still wearing a tuxedo likely stole from the Skirvin Hotel. He stopped, looked up at the board to check that the early bird *Ace in the Hole* flight to Las Vegas was scheduled to load up at Gate 8, then set down right across from her and looked at his pocketwatch.

"I reckon you're anxious as a White Rabbit to get back down into your rightful hole," she said to him. "But it won't do you no good, 'cause you won't be staying in Vegas for long, due to what happened here in OKC."

"*Que*?" he replied, with a startled look in his unHispanic blue eyes. "No *hablo* English."

"I spotted a picture of you in a press kit: Standing right next to the baldheaded **Farmers** Guy at last year's Fritos. But you're naturally light-haired, so I didn't recognize who you are 'til I saw how you reacted last night to the famous emcee not wanting you to hand out that loaded Frito to Mr. Mayhem. You are none other than Henry P. Friedlander alright, Assistant Manager of the Wonderland Hotel & Casino."

"So what?" he said in plain English. "I've been scouting the competition, incognito: Checking out what to do—and what <u>not</u> to do—when hosting a big league event such as the Fritos. I now have nothing to hide. The Academy has already announced it's wise decision to return the TVC Awards to Wonderland."

"'Likely in part due to your own dern mischief! I reckon it was you who put out those anonymous death threats, and did every random foul thing you could think of to make OKC look unglamorous."

"You Okies and your paranoia!" he snorted. "Shit happens, especially in this dirt-ball corner of the world. Read today's newspapers: Your own Mayor says he's relieved the Fritos are not coming back here. It wasn't me who made OKC look 'unglamorous'. This minor league town was born that way."

"The Mayor won't talk to me, and I missed the deadline again by the time I got my own big newspaper story put together and sent in. But my boss said he would pass it on to his Honor, so…"

"Again, so what? You have no proof I was behind any 'mischief'. Didn't you see that award-winning spot that incriminated the short Mafia hit man and the two godfathers?"

"I happen to know that it was my own dern mother, Wynona Sue, who passed on to the F.B.I. a tall tale told by Mr. Deano that incriminated Ms. Clo, which is no doubt why she turned the table on him in the hotel bar. I also know what a gal by the name of Shirley Parker told me last night after that firecracker you tried to hand to Mr. Mayhem semi-exploded."

"Who the hell is Shirley Parker?"

"She's a gal who has also been working incognito, under the name 'Dana Clack', who told me how you led Mr. Mayhem up to that eleventh-floor ledge."

"He wanted to go up there, and was—or is—notoriously clumsy."

"You and her set up the head table for the Hall of Fame induction banquet, and knew that poor old Mrs. Fletcher had acid reflux of the bowels. Ms. Shirley admits to spitting **Brown Wad** chewing tobacco juice on a meatball that got put on William Shatner's plate by mistake. I reckon it was you who squirted **Tabasco** sauce onto the partial one Mrs. Fletcher ate."

"Ha! No way would any Nevada court extradite me back to this grease spot on the map based on anything you or that crazy kitchen woman 'reckons'."

"And now I my own self realize that after you stuck your head into that mini-elevator shaft connected to a Venetian Room and no doubt saw the **Farmers** Insurance Guy's bald head coming up at you, you heard him holler he had figured out what you did, maybe after recognizing you from last year's Frito Awards. There was nothing '*loco*' about the dumbwaiter's mechanical operation 'til you turned off the light and pushed that button to make it fall back down the shaft."

"Due to your Mayor's insane rantings, anyone in my place would have feared old baldy was mounting a hot gravy attack on the OKC **Sonic** 'Guy', who was supposed to be at the party. Your own Chief of Police gave me a pat on the back."

"I reckon it was you your own self who was up to causing trouble at the party with that kettle of hot gravy. As for that loaded Frito…"

Flight 777, the early bird Ace in the Hole to Las Vegas, is now ready for boarding.

"Who would believe that I—of all people—would risk setting Mr. Las Vegas's face on fire? It's the…the face of my own glamorous big league city, for cryin' out loud," said the mischief maker, getting up from his seat. "By now, you Okies ought to know when you're beat."

"We ain't beat," Henrietta said, standing up her own self and and getting into the out-of-towner's face, which—to judge by the wild look that came into his blue eyes —seemed to unspool Henry Friedlander. "Not by a long shot."

"Oh yeah," he said, hovering over her like an angry dark storm cloud. "We took the **National Finals Rodeo** from you, almost got your Cowboy Hall of Fame on our first try, and we're not done yet. Next we're gonna steal your Thunder," he said, no doubt referring to the professional basketball team that OKC semi-stole from Seattle, "plus your fine zoo, including that stuffed leopard; and that Indian statue on top of your Capitol building, to boot. Just for fun, we might even..."

Boarding of Flight 777 has been delayed by order of local authorities.

As the boastful Las Vegas booster looked past her, Henrietta saw the fiery pride in his eyes turn to cowardly fear. She turned around and...Here came the Mayor, the Chief of Police, and some other local authorities in uniform; blustering down the airport concourse like, well, like wind sweeping down the Plain after a hard rain.

THE
END

Made in the USA
Las Vegas, NV
22 February 2026

42433123R00115